The Accidental Alpha

RJ Berryhill

ISBN: 979-8-218-77496-7

Edited By: DerpyWickedFox Editorial

Cover: NK Winter

Map: @SaumyasVision

Content Warnings

This book contains G!P, knotting, descriptions of heat and mating. It has explicit scene between two women and one while pregnant. Pregnancy is a big theme during this book. If you are unfamiliar with these terms, there is an omegaverse encyclopedia on my Instagram @RJ_Berryhillauthor. If any of these themes make you uncomfortable this book is not for you.

Author's Note

Please note I updated the name of a minor side character who appears late in the narrative. Recently I was made aware that the character's former name has historically been used as a slur against Jewish people. The manuscript was immediately updated. I failed to research the character name and was unaware of the history of the slur. The action was ignorant and harmful, and I deeply apologize for the harm it has caused to any of my readers. Going forward I will be more aware and thoroughly research.

Whaow Frar
Jaeredale
Atesa
Sutherland
The Ruins of Luiza
Royal Palace
Nuvona
Rererwallow
Trilla
Ruins of Kilfall

Chapter 1

Dove really regretted being in a room full of Alphas when her heat was about to start. The most infuriating of them all, though, was the captain of the army who she shared a best friend with—the Queen.

She had known her for over ten years, but even now Dove found her insufferable as she walked around with that straight spine and proud smirk. Like she just fucked multiple women.

Her knot was probably tiny.

Yet as she walked by Dove, light gold springy curls falling at her waist while green eyes fluttered around the room, Dove couldn't help but breathe in her scent. She smelled like oak and honeysuckles, sweet but intoxicating. Her scent made no sense when it came to her demeanor. She walked around like the proud Alpha she was, but her smell was sweet while always holding an undertone of insecurity.

Dove rolled her eyes as she watched her—May Charlotte. She would never let anyone call her by her full name. But May...she was the biggest, most untamed Alpha around, and there she stood across the ballroom, tempting Dove.

Dove would admit she fell victim to May charm during their younger years. It was almost impossible not to when the Alphas whole existence was to find and fuck other women. It was only then she realized May didn't care about Dove the same way she did. Not beyond someone she could make out and flirt with as they never slept together. That teenage heartbreak was why she hated her now.

With their connection of a shared best friend, Dove's heartbreak had crystallized into a form of hatred and sensitivity that helped her keep May at arm's length, as if she would shatter all over again.

Pushing aside the disdain towards her first kiss, and Alpha who had broken her heart, she straightened the white lace shawl that hung around her emerald dress. Dove watched May stroll across the room to their best friend. As Captain, May had to make sure Her Highness was okay.

The royal wedding belonged to her best friend and Queen, Taylor Atwood. The wedding ceremony had commenced earlier and now she and the bride, Eveleen, were dancing.

While Dove was Taylor's true best friend and was in front row for the wedding party, she now sat with the kitchen staff, making sure her food went out appropriately. The only thing she hated was the shawl around her throat, but she used it to stop her pheromones from spreading into the room.

The fabric rubbed against Dove's prickled skin as sweat warmed her body. Her heat was coming up fast as she watched the plate of food she had prepared earlier. Nothing could help her now.

Dove's pheromones were bleeding into every inch of the ballroom, seeping into every Alpha around. Of course, the Betas and Omegas could smell it too, but only the Alphas were truly affected by the heat coming from her body. The need to be taken, the need to be rutted and knotted was slowly overpowering her mind. She could sense a few Alphas invading her space, trying to use their own pheromones to claim her.

Dove would not be claimed.

Music continued to fill the room, but none of it reached Dove's ears as her gaze slowly turned blurry.

She felt like a small fish in a pond of sharks the longer her body released pheromones. One of the Alphas on staff floated towards her as she stood.

Glancing over to May who was whispering in Taylor's ear, May caught Dove's eye. Her green gaze bore into Dove's soul, and her clothes began to itch at her skin from the intensity of it. It was like May could read into the deepest part of her soul, like the Alpha could sense exactly what she needed from all the way across the room. She saw a slight tug on her lips and decided it was time to leave.

Passing the tray on to another servant, Dove exited the ballroom, stumbling along the chestnut hallways slowly to her family's floor.

For almost 200 years, Dove's kin had served the royal family. The two families had known each other for as long as their country had been settled. The country of Whaow Frar had only ever existed under Taylor's family. It had been founded by their ancestors and settled together. Ever since then Dove's family had been loyal to the throne.

Dove's room—a deep maroon with a four-poster bed in the middle of it—had always been her sanctuary. But not even its familiarity could rid her of the discomfort raging through her. The fire had died long ago, and with the oncoming body heat, Dove practically ripped her balcony doors open.

Stripping the emerald dress off her skin, Dove threw it across the room. The clothes that were dirty had to be cleaned soon anyways. Her breasts were exposed to the air as she took a deep breath. Her heats had been getting stronger and longer as she grew older. Her Omega was craving pups.

She hadn't found an Alpha she loved and wanted to mate, but that was a small dream of Dove's. Her logical mind knew that one day she would, but as every heat passed, she needed a mate and a pup.

Pressing her forehead to the fur on the bed, Dove stripped her breast band off. A prison on her skin meant nothing more than to restrict her nature. She had not had an Alpha to guide her through her heat in such a long time. She felt her Omega wailing inside her as everything around her became too much. She needed an Alpha, and only one came to her mind.

Sweat ran down her forehead, dropping into a lonely pool at her feet. A beat was pulsing in her ears as she watched the pool grow. A thrum of an insistent beating. Her body slowly began dissolving, breaking, as every nerve in her begged to be fucked.

"Dove?" There were three simple knocks on her door. "Dovely, are you okay?"

She pushed her hands against her ears to stop the overwhelming beating of her heart. May was the only person who was allowed to call her by her birth name, the one her parents gave her as a newborn pup. When anyone else called her Dovely, she got aggravated. But when May did it, it felt like honey on her lips and a soft whisper in her ear. It flowed so smoothly off May's tongue, and as infuriating as she found May, Dove desired her name on her lips.

With gritted teeth, Dove forced out her words. "Leave, May."

"I can scent you through the door, Dove. You either let me in, or I will break it down." May was always so aggressive, which helped with her nature as a captain, but Dove couldn't handle it right now. As annoying as she found her, Dove's Omega sometimes craved her. She was gorgeous after all, with her springy almost-white curls that reached all the way down to her waist and even though she had a few visible scars, her skin looked as soft as her finest furs. Those dark green eyes were always looking for trouble but softened when she saw Dove. She was, by definition, the perfect specimen.

"If you can scent me then go. You know that." She grabbed the furs in her hands, her knees digging into the floor. May's scent penetrated her nose through the door, sweet like the flower and earthy as oak. Her favorite thing.

***

"Dove? Let me inside. Your scent is creating a storm in me." A low growl echoed in the hall as May tried to crack the door to address her friend. "Dove?" It wasn't like May hadn't seen Dove naked before, but this was different.

May's Alpha was waiting to be released onto her Omega. She could feel Dove's Omega flaring to life, begging to be knotted. May had never witnessed Dove's heat being this intense. May had been close to Dove every day since they met. There were few days that they were apart, and that was only when Taylor had to leave the safety of their castle. As her army Captain, May spent a lot of time around Taylor, and since Dove was her best friend, she was always there in proximity.

May had always had this intense need to make sure Dove was safe at all times. She knew what Dove thought about her, and maybe that helped May stay at arm's length, because the truth was, she would drop on her sword for Dove. There was no Omega in the world who could compare to Dove. She was stubborn and insubordinate, with the liberty of being friends with the Queen, and May loved that about her. Dove knew her place in the world. She didn't mind that her family were staff to the throne. Dove stood her ground and her morals. It was everything May wanted in a mate, but there was more too.

Dove's beauty couldn't compare. Her hair burned brighter than the sun. The orange in her locks weaved well with the few brown streaks that came out during the summer. Loose waves that May wanted to run her fingers through and yet clutch with her fist while she took Dove from behind.

Her eyes had captivated May since day one, though. Dove wore every emotion on her face, her heart on her sleeve, and her eyes were the window to her soul. Those hazel eyes that had a hint of gold in the middle were a lighthouse for May's stormy days. While Dove believed she didn't have the perfect figure, she was the final puzzle piece for May. If only she could get over herself and be the Alpha Dove deserved, but right now Dove needed her.

"May, if you don't leave right now, we're both going to do something we regret."

May pushed her Alpha down. She couldn't let it take control when Dove was in a vulnerable state. With each passing second, though, she had to fight from ripping the door off its hinges and giving Dove whatever she desired. Her body, her knot, her heart, Dove could have it all.

"I would never regret you," May murmured, hoping Dove was too preoccupied to hear. May pressed her head against the oak door, getting ready to return to the ceremony when Dove let out a harsh wail. A howl of pain which soared right past May's defenses and brought her Alpha front and center.

Shoving the door open, she found Dove sitting on her knees with her head buried into the fur on her bed. Her sun-kissed skin was red, glistening with sweat. The halo of hair was a disarray of flyaway strands and soaked with sweat. But her pheromones were the worst for May. She was in distress, her Omega overtaking every one of her senses and locking up the Dove she loved. May did not know what it was like to be in heat, but she was told that the emptiness inside an Omega caused them physical pain. They needed to be taken by Alphas to satiate the pain.

May tried to calm Dove with her own scent, but it was no use. When Dove turned her head to look at May, only one eye was visible through the curtain of hair.

"May, please..."

It wasn't a 'please leave' like the last few but a 'please help me.' Dove needed her. Her Omega was howling inside her, in pain as she stared at the Alpha. May's Alpha flared to life with the singular word and the sweet berry smell coming from Dove. She always smelled so sweet. Like honey and the finest wild berries. She had always wondered if Dove's freckled skin was as pleasant as the smell.

"I will take care of you, my Dove. Tell me what you need." May stepped further into the room and realized the fire wasn't lit. She grabbed a few logs to throw on while regaining control of her Alpha once again. This would not be a passionless fuck between her and a random Omega. This would not be a rutting session to release her frustration. No, this would be her helping the woman she loved through a fierce heat. Her royal duty may be to the queen, but her number one loyalty was to her sweet Dove.

Chapter 2

Dove's breath released in an almost content sigh when May entered the room. The Alpha's pheromones were coming off in waves, wrapping around her and her Omega. Whether May realized it or not, Dove couldn't tell. Her own pheromones were going crazy. Begging, pleading, and needing to be taken. To be given the knot of the Alpha nearby and craving her seed. Her illogical mind even craved May's pups. She was nearing twenty-nine, after all.

The fire roared to life as Dove continued burying her head into the fur. She knew that she and May were going to have sex as soon as she entered the room. The throbbing grew low in her belly until her clit had its own heartbeat. Her lower body was warm with desire, ready to have May inside her. Her Omega needed to be taken by the Alpha just across the room.

Then a thought hit her. A thought that clenched her heart so hard she started to dry heave. She couldn't manage to eat during the reception and now she was glad she didn't. Calloused hands held back her hair as she gagged towards the floor.

"I have got you, Dovely." Then unlike the calloused grip, a gentle hand ran down her shoulder blade. "It will be okay." As much as Dove wanted to wrench away, she melted. Dove's primal urge to satisfy her Omega was being filled. She knew that May was a giver, and she was devoting her attention, until she remembered why she started dry heaving.

"You fucked her." Dove's voice broke as she wiped the back of her mouth with her hand. "I saw you leave the ballroom with *her*." She tried to shrug May's hands off, but they were the only thing grounding her. The heat continued to overwhelm her.

"What? Dove, what are you talking about?" The scents in the room were now a mix of confusion and sadness that Dove wasn't entirely able to understand alongside her own feelings. Her Omega clawed every inch of her skin, making its escape.

"That Beta." To emphasize her point, she spat on the ground and got the final bit of acid out. May's hands retreated from her body. The warming pheromones that reminded her of home quickly left the air.

May wasn't necessarily angry, but she wasn't happy at the accusation either. Of course she wasn't!

"Dove, I..." May trailed off, confirming Dove's assumption. She decided now was the time to climb on her bed. The trunk at the end of the bed was somewhat getting in her way but May held her hips as she crawled up. The simple gesture relit the heat in her body. Her nipples were aching against the air, and her clit pulsed to life. Every nerve ending stood on high alert when the Alpha touched her, and the hand to skin contact made Dove slick with arousal.

"Was she everything you wanted? Did she feel full around you, May?" Consciously, Dove wasn't trying to make her angry, but maybe her Omega needed the Alpha to come to life. She needed to know that May would fight for her. That she wanted Dove just as much as she craved May. The satin sheets just made her skin burn. The sweat was now a field around her body. She heard May scoff and saw her look at the ground.

"You have no idea."

"What? I have no idea what it's like to be fucked senseless? To feel a cock buried so deep inside me that I lose all my control? I do, May, so fuck you." Dove pulled her hair, trying to redirect the pain of her empty pulsing pussy to anywhere else. The little sting of pain in her scalp offset the deep throb of her lower extremities. Her slick burned down her thighs as May moved away, backing away from Dove, her scent now mostly aggravated. Dove would have been curious as to why, but she was preoccupied with the second skin of sweat she had.

"Do not say that," May growled. She hardly ever showed any aggression towards Dove, and even now with the low angry rumble showed she wasn't upset with Dove.

"Say what? That *you* fucked her senseless? That your cock was buried in her? Because I know you have. Many times. You don't want an Omega. You don't want someone to love, May. You just want a body."

Dove didn't know why she was tempting the big Alpha. But she wanted the Alpha to show her what she was made of. May had always been so tame around her. Dove hated it.

But May's Alpha burned to life from what Dove said. Dove could see May's need to remind her, the Omega, that she was the more dominant one between them, but May seemed to push it down.

"I have not fucked anyone in over a year, Dovely. The only gratification I have had is from myself." She neared Dove, whose Omega purred in response. May was the biggest womanizer around, but now that Dove found out she hadn't had sex in a year, her heart skipped a beat.

Dove also knew that May had had a rut in the past year. She remembered when Taylor had mentioned that May was occupied that week. Did May deal with that alone?

"If you do not believe me then I will leave and let you deal with your heat alone. Otherwise, tell your Alpha what you need."

Dove couldn't resist; she turned to see the golden hair goddess with her ceremonial uniform cascading down her body. The deep navy always brought out the soft tones in May's paler skin, but right now she wanted it off.

Laying herself on her back, Dove's legs slowly parted. She still had her braies on and the dark stain was visible. They were made of a thin linen, so her slick started leaking through. May stood at the edge of the bed, pride on her face. A low growl filled the room, barely audible above the crackling in the fire. She was still hesitating. They both were. Even with their primal urges, and the need begging them to go at it, they both knew this would change them forever. Dove didn't know if she was ready for that, and May seemed to sense it. Right now, though, it didn't matter, not when Dove's heat broke her.

The pulsing in her body became its own heartbeat, clawing her from the inside out and making her arch off the bed. Even though her chest was bare, it was as if a thousand tiny pins were prickling her skin. Her body was a cage and only May had the key. She could barely hear the Alpha over the thrumming in her ears.

"Dove? Just tell me what you need. Tell me, my sweet Dove." May had moved on the bed, her uniform had been shed to the floor and all that remained was a soft white tunic.

Dove turned to her with the tears in her eyes. Clawing her bedspread, she resisted pulling the rest of May's clothes off and directing her where she needed most.

"Please May..." Tears burned her cheeks. "I need you, all of you." She surrendered to her Omega. This was all she needed.

"I got you Dovely. I will give you everything." May crawled over to Dove and her thighs finally bracketed Dove's hips. Dove felt the friction through May's clothes and pushed her stomach up, trying to get more. A groan escaped both of them. May stripped all her garments off, so she was finally revealing herself to Dove, except her own braies.

"I will give it to you, but I am going to kiss those sweet lips first." May's muscular figure bent over Dove with her hands on either side of her head, careful not to hurt her. With one final act, she pushed Dove's fiery hair to the side, her lips descending in what felt like an eternity to Dove. When they met hers, everything in her body stopped. The vibration, the pulsing, the sweat all came to nothing. Dove's hands instantly buried themselves in May's hair, pulling her closer because it wasn't enough. She wanted to feel May's entire body on her.

"More," Dove pleaded. May tilted her head just a little so her tongue could swipe at Dove's bottom lip, and when their tongues connected, the Alpha started to present herself to Dove.

May's hard length rubbed against Dove's braies, where the wet heat of her body pooled. Her slick gushed out, soaking the sheets under her. May lowered her body so their skin finally touched, and Dove's needy whimper broke free in response. She almost came at the touch of their bodies but shivered instead as May's bare breasts brushed against Dove's hardened nipples.

Breaking the kiss, Dove let out a moan from deep within her. May took the opportunity to move her lips down Dove's jaw. Tilting her head to the side, she felt May's hands grasp her swollen nipples and pinch them.

During her heat her breasts grew, along with her nipples. She typically needed a more sensitive touch to them, but it was like May was in tune with every vibration in her body. The soft kisses skating her jaw were just what Dove needed to help calm her raging desire.

"You taste so sweet, Dovely. Like honey," May grunted out as she nipped Dove's neck, right above her scent gland, releasing a low grumble next to her ear. Dove grabbed a handful of the silky golden curls, pulling her closer. Almost every point of their bodies were touching. Her Omega whined, almost begging May to bite her. To make her the only one for May. May's scent would be attached to Dove's Omega for all time.

"More," Dove gasped in a strangled voice when May continued with another pinch at her nipple. Dove needed May to take her most intimate area.

"How about we get these off of you." May hooked her fingers into the braies at Dove's hips, yanking down the final barrier on Dove. "So I can see how your pussy tastes compared to your skin." Dove's half-hooded eyes captured hers and May licked her lips.

It was the sexiest thing Dove ever witnessed. The way May looked down at her glistening pussy as if she were the finest meal in the world. Dove hardly noticed the clench of May's jaw as her own hand wandered down her body. Letting her hand pass by her nipples, she continued south.

"No. You are not to touch your pretty pink pussy unless I tell you to." May grabbed her hand as fast it wandered, pinning it above Dove's head. The Alpha leaned down, her breath barely an inch from Dove's mouth, whose gaze shifted to the fire. The smoky scent bleeding into the room couldn't be scented over their mixing pheromones. Somewhere between her looking at the fire, May stripped off her bottoms, leaving her fully naked. Her cock sprang to life, pre-come glistening the head. Dove saw May's own secondary entrance glistening with arousal but ignored it. She was too distracted by the hard veiny cock, ready to take it in her mouth. She wanted May to thrust into her mouth until she came, spilling down her throat.

"Do you understand, my Omega." One of May's sandy eyebrows twitched upward, daring Dove to be disobedient. In any other circumstance Dove would never let another tell her what she couldn't do during sex, but this was different. The Alpha in front of her was demanding obedience. Dove's Omega could hardly disagree when her green eyes were filled with lust as they glanced down at the slick coating her thighs. More pre-come dribbled from May's cock.

Dove would do anything to have it in her.

"Yes, Alpha." Uttering the words was so easy. It was like she was made to whisper them to May. She felt her barriers lower when May's lips pulled into the slightest smile.

"Good girl, Dovely. Now you are going to watch while I eat your pussy and if you look away for even a second, I will leave you on your own." All Dove could manage to do was swallow when May leaned down to kiss her once more. Fireworks danced behind her eyes with each brush of their lips.

May's fingers danced slowly under Dove's breast. She gripped it a bit too tightly, causing Dove to let out a pained moan. Retracting her hand and lips, May met Dove's gaze.

"Dove, if this is too much we can stop. There are other things I have heard of that satiate Omegas in heat for a while. I can draw a bath for you or—" Dove didn't let her finish, claiming her lips in a ravenous manner.

"I want you, May. I *need* you. Your touch, your body, and your knot are all that can help me now. Only you, May," Dove choked out the words before May slowly dipped down with a brush of a kiss before pressing their foreheads together. "Just be soft please. My heat makes me extra sensitive." While it was true, she also wanted May to take her hard, but she needed delicate touches right now.

"Tell me what you need, Dovely. Never stop telling me." May's words stroked Dove's Omega. She whimpered a broken *yes*, before they continued moving together like one well-oiled machine. As if their bodies were made for each other.

"If you are ready, Dove, I am dying to taste you." The idea of May licking her pussy, sucking her clit almost drove her sensitive body to the edge. She was so close to getting that talented tongue on her, that it felt like a dream. A noise escaped her at the thought. Here was someone she despised yet someone she needed more than anyone at this moment.

"May, yes Gods! I need to feel you on me."

Before Dove could process what was happening, May's breath tingled with the heat radiating from her pussy. She felt a few delicate kisses press onto her thighs, where her only stretch marks lived.

"These are so beautiful. I remember the first time I saw them. I wanted to kiss them right then and there.

Drop to my knees and worship what you think is every imperfection, because you Dovely, are faultless, flawless, and every word to describe perfection." Her heartbeat was the only thing she heard with May's words, but she wouldn't think about it now.

"I need you inside me, May." Her pussy clenched around nothing, a spasm in her walls because she was empty.

"I am going to give you everything." May moved in and finally placed an excruciatingly small kiss on the lips of Dove's pussy. "One." Another higher up. "Kiss." Another. "At a time."

Dove's slick coated her inner thighs and the lips of her pussy. She had to resist pressing her legs together to ease some of the tension. Her arousal pooled out and May captured it on her tongue.

"Keep these legs nice and open for me. You can only stop holding them when your thighs squeeze my head as you scream my name." May dove into her heat, her face covering Dove's most intimate area. May sucked all her slick up as Dove pressed off the bed, moaning. She tried to stay still while May licked at her and reached up to toy with her nipple. Her body was more sensitive than before, but it still felt glorious. Just one flick sent tremors through her chest.

"Gods, Dovely. You taste even better than I imagined." While May's tongue poked into her opening, a finger brushed against her hardened clit.

"May." Dove's voice broke as May's finger sped up as she moaned against her, the vibration pushing her off the edge. Shaking under May's passion, slick flooded her body and set every nerve of her skin on fire.

Dove had never had an orgasm overtake every sense of her body, but as May ate her out like heaven's food, her brain went into overdrive. Everywhere May touched sent her to a new level of pleasure. Her Alpha was giving her everything she required. She had never been this pleased when she collapsed on the bed, a broken Omega. But still her heat wasn't satiated. She needed May's knot.

Chapter 3

Dove was ready.

Her sweet arousal glistened on her thighs and pooled around her pussy. May took some of her pre-come and wiped it on her tip. Rolling her shoulders back, she positioned herself between Dove's legs and ran her length between Dove's lips.

May's heart stuttered. She was so close to having her Dove. She paused for just a moment to see Dove throw her head back, pinching her own nipples. Her mouth was open like a silent scream, even though May wasn't even an inch in.

"Dove? Is this okay?" Her Omega nodded in response, her eyelids heavy, but May needed a verbal confirmation.

"I need the words, Dovely."

"Yes, May. Goddess, please give me your knot. I need you to fill me already." With that, May grabbed Dove's leg so she could slide right in. Pushing past the entrance bit by bit, May had to resist the urge to come right there.

This is where she belonged. She had craved this Omega since before she could even remember. When she started growing taller than May, only for May to have her own growth spurt. When Dove wore trousers for the first time as she rode, and tonight when Dove had an emerald gown on. May had been desperate to wrap her hands around the shawl and pound into her. But also desperate to help straighten it because Dove wouldn't. That's what May was. Desperate. So she pushed all her thoughts aside to enjoy the moment and inched forward.

Dove's breath was a shudder as May pushed in. Velvety heat engulfed her cock, causing May to drop Dove's legs to compose herself as Dove's hungry pussy continued to pull her length in. It was home. Her Alpha was begging to mark every inch of the Omega's skin. She bowed her head slightly as Dove's walls tightened. She was almost halfway in but she could feel her knot forming. She would not come until Dove did. Opening her eyes and locking them with Dove's, she continued.

"Please May. Please. Fill me. Fuck me. Knot me." Her words were almost a shout as Dove's hands raised to grab her arms. May nodded and in one move, buried herself all the way into Dove, feeling herself pressing into the deepest part of the Omega. May could barely move as Dove's inner walls squeezed her.

"You're so big. I can feel you stretching me."

May could feel it too. She was whole as Dove's body pulled her in. Tears formed in her eyes, but she pushed them aside.

"Do you want me to wait a minute or are you ready?" All May wanted was to claim every inch of Dove. She wanted Dove to scream her name and tell the world how perfect May was. How good she felt when May took care of her. May almost became a whimpering mess when she felt a slight squeeze around her length, and a shuddering breath fell from her lips.

"I need a minute please."

"Okay, but I need to shift a bit." May bent her body over slightly to relieve some of the pressure the angle was creating. Dove ran her fingers up and down May's arm, a soft trail of her fingertips, before May's need to kiss her overwhelmed her as she bent down to claim Dove's lips. Once she started thrusting, her Alpha would come out. She could only do so much to stop herself, so she craved for one more moment.

When May dipped closer to Dove, she realized that Dove was purring. She hadn't even moved or come yet and Dove was *purring*. It vibrated deep in May's soul. She pressed a kiss tenderly to Dove's lips, brushing her lips along Dove's jaw as she did before. May nipped lightly at her ears, which prompted Dove to release a little gasp. Her scent gland was right below it, calling to her. It would be so easy to break her skin and take Dove as her mate.

The thought filled her mind. Dove would smell like her, and all the other Alphas would know that Dove was hers. Dove would be hers. Her mate. She wanted that so badly, but she would never do that unless Dove wanted it too, no matter how much her Alpha cried.

"I am going to move now, Dovely." Moving onto her knees, she took Dove's legs again and slowly pulled out. Dove clawed her furs in response as the obscene sound of their most sensitive parts filled the room. May's throat ran dry when she was almost all the way out. She glanced down at her cock, admiring the way it was covered in

Dove's arousal. Dove must've known what she was thinking because more slick dribbled out of her pussy.

"Take me Alpha." May thrust all the way back into Dove. Dove's mouth fell open and gaped further as May started to pull back out, creating a rhythm of rocking her hips back and forth. The bed creaked as Dove's pants grew, and May's growls intensified. Dove wrapped her legs around May while she moved her hips at an impossible speed. She grunted when Dove's arms reached up to claw her shoulders. Her hips moved faster, the sound of their bodies slapping together echoing through the room. A shiver ran down May's spine when she realized the pants in the room were from her Omega. She was making Dove cry in pleasure each time her hips slapped Dove's ass.

"Tell me, Dove. Tell me how it feels." She knew Dove liked the dirty talk because the walls of her pussy fluttered. She almost stopped her motion when she felt her orgasm build. Her knot was almost fully formed when Dove answered.

"You feel like magic. You're so big and you stretch me so well. I love the feeling of you buried inside me." Dove spoke as her eyebrows formed a line of pleasure.

The column of her throat looked delicious. May leaned down and ran her lips along it as she continued her movements, her knot fully formed.

"I want your knot, Alpha. Knot me, please." May was beyond words. She almost never used words during sex, but she wanted to with Dove. However, nothing could be said for how immaculate she felt with her being inside Dove. They were joined together as close as two people could be.

May surged forward. Her knot had always been big; she could only imagine how that would feel to Dove.

"*Oh.*" Dove's words barely registered as her knot slipped in, the pop sounding. When she felt that final connection, Dove started writhing under her. "I-I'm coming, oh f-fuck. May!" She screamed May's name over and over again, locking her legs around the Alpha's back and leaving claw marks that would last for days.

May couldn't stop it when her come burst into Dove. She felt spurt after spurt release as her knot kept them together. Her seed was in Dove, mixing with Dove's come. They both knew they would be locked together for a while.

May collapsed against Dove. Her forehead rested against Dove's shoulder whose content purr continued. May ran her head back and forth against Dove shoulder, breathing in her scent. The whole room smelled like them. Like sex.

She had sex with Dove. May drove Dove wild with purrs, growls and screaming. She finally felt what it was like to have Dove's pussy grip her. To feel her inner walls with each thrust. To be able to come inside her and be tied together with her knot. How would she ever be able to go back to the way it was before?

After her knot deflated, she was getting ready to pull out of Dove when a hand wrapped around her lower waist. The Omega was still purring below her prompting May to nuzzle Dove's neck. This was everything she wanted in life. When she saw Dove, it was like a ray of sunlight after a storm. She was now connected to Dove in every way she could be except as her mate, which was something she dreamed about constantly.

"Can we just lie like this for a minute?" Dove's whisper brushed her neck. "Will you put your weight on me May, please? I want to feel all of you."

"I do not want to hurt you, Dovely." May drew her face up, still barely hovering above Dove on her elbows. She could barely add the next part about her cock shifting deeper in Dove, before she was pulled down. With her fully settled on Dove's pelvis, and their breasts mashed together, May's cock sprang to life again.

"Oh fuck!"

May's nose dove into Dove's mating gland to nip at it. She knew that Dove would catch on to her obsession with the gland, but she couldn't stop the gravitational pull she felt. She never loved anyone like she did Dove.

"May, I never knew you could feel this good." May ignored the slight sting of her words and instead kept up her attack at the crease of Dove's neck and shoulder. The scent coming off of her smelled faintly of May now that her come was in the Omega. May couldn't resist biting. It wasn't enough to mate them, but it was enough for Dove to grab the back of her head. May couldn't see it, but she could feel Dove throwing her head back. May lavished the rest of her attack in gentle kisses before finally accepting that she was full-on lying on top of Dove.

After a few minutes of resting together, Dove finally urged May to pull out.

"Will you hold me?" Dove whimpered her words while her red hair tickled May's nose. Dove's arms still hugged May's lower waist, who rolled them on her back carefully. Dove snuggled closer into May's chest, who's breasts were almost framing Dove's face. Most of her body was limp and relaxed now, but having the woman she loved in her arms, while her heat pheromones flooded her nose, almost sent her into a rut. She gently rubbed her hands up and down Dove's freckled body before pressing her lips to Dove's forehead.

"Was that okay?" May was suddenly self-conscious that she didn't perform well enough for Dove. She had never been with an Omega in heat before because there was only one she wanted. Dove's scent screamed relaxed and content, but May was always doubting herself.

"That was exactly what I needed." Dove pulled her head up to rest her chin on May's collarbone. Her hazel eyes glowed with admiration before trailing her finger across May's shoulder. Her Omega was still guided by her heat, but May would soak up every moment she could with Dove.

"Do you need to get back to the reception?" The finger continued feathering her skin lightly, and May couldn't help but shiver.

"I alerted Caleb that I might be unreachable for the evening." Dove rolled her beautiful eyes, which brought giggles to burst from May. She placed her hand on the dimple in Dove's lower back. "Of course I did not expect for this, but I thought I may have to guard you from one or more territorial Alphas who would approach a vulnerable Omega."

Dove arched a fiery eyebrow that was surrounded by her freckles. Even though she was trying to keep her smirk at play, her dimples glowed in the light.

"Protect me, huh?" Dove ducked and placed a kiss between May's breasts, causing a single pulse in her cock. May could scent the slick that was building in the Omega's swollen pussy.

"I would never think you needed protection, but those Alphas were circling you."

"So, what you're saying is that you don't need to be there for the rest of Taylor's reception?" The hopeful words escaped Dove's swollen puffy lips. This may have been as close to groveling that Dove had done in front of

May. The suddenly shy Omega tucked her head towards May's breasts, and a warm breath brushed one of her dusty brown nipples.

"If you would like me to stay here tonight, Dovely, then just ask me, please." She needed to hear the words from her Omega. She knew there was no hope for the two of them, but spending a night with Dove was everything she dreamed of.

"Would you please stay with me?"

"Yes Dovely. I will stay." Dove's smile lit up every cell in May's body. The Omega crawled up a few inches, bringing their lips together in a fiery kiss. May kissed her back with everything she could, almost crying that she got the chance to hold her, the only woman she ever loved.

Chapter 4

Dove had no idea how long they had lain together, cuddled up before she fell asleep. Feeling the Alpha come inside of her had been enough to sate her heat for a while, but it would come back in full swing with time. They hadn't spoken much while Dove lay with her head on May's generous chest. Even though the captain spent most of her hours in metal or training, her breasts were glorious. Dove knew ever since they had been young adults that May was self-conscious about the size of her breasts, but Dove had always found them irresistible.

Eventually the fire had dwindled, but Dove was still craving it. When her heat first came on, she'd opened the balcony doors to get some cool air, but now with the lack of fire and strong wind, she was chilly. She didn't even have to say anything before May pulled the blanket over her before getting up to close the doors. Once she did, Dove breathed out an audible sigh of relief.

"Does that feel better?" May's completely naked body was standing in front of the doors. The moonlight hit her light blonde hair and accented her curves. How had Dove never totally noticed the perfection of May's body? She had a few battle scars, but no other imperfections. Though Dove never thought of the scars that way because they were proof of how much of a survivor May was. She knew all of May's history, so she would never believe otherwise.

"I'm still chilly. Could you light up a small fire please?" Her Omega had always been incredibly needy during her heat. She never imagined that having sex with May would satiate her desire almost completely. Dove could feel the burning heat still present in her chest, but right now she never felt more peaceful during one. She gripped the blanket tighter around her body as May moved towards the fire. Her cock was the right size for her body, and Dove's. Nothing had ever made her feel so full, so perfectly stuffed. The veins on the shaft ran up to May's abdomen and the tip was the prettiest shade of pink. Dove bit her lips as May bent down to grab some of the firewood Dove had stashed next to her hearth.

"Your pheromones are giving you away, Dovely." May's taut ass had a birthmark on it, as she remained bent over to light the fire. She lit the spark almost instantly before gathering Dove's empty chalice and filling it with water. Dove shifted her head slightly to the side as she watched. How had she never realized how caring May was? Even as she furiously fucked Dove, each question she breathed was filled with concerned. She wanted Dove to feel safe and secure with each stroke inside her.

"I can't help it when you're bent over like that. Your cock dangling between your legs while your flawless ass is on display, plus your curls are falling all over your body. It's the best blend of flawlessness I've seen in a while." Dove lay on her side while the blanket covered most of her upper body. She held her fingers out to frame the naked body in front of her. May let out the lightest chuckle when she caught Dove's dramatic display, warming Dove's heart. The tall Alpha turned around to her full height, causing Dove's throat to dry and slick to build in her core. She could already feel the singular pulse in her clit as May approached, bending down to give her a chaste kiss. The gentleness in her kiss scared off her heat more.

"I thought you wanted to rest for a while?" May stopped a few inches away from her lips, while both of her hands rested on the edge of the bed. White blonde hair spilled over May's shoulders, brushing over her forearms. She was undeniably and effortlessly sexy. She was everything Dove wanted.

Dove's hands shot out to bring May back in for a kiss. A deep moan burst from her chest as the passion of her kiss bled out. She swiped her tongue along May's lips. She could tell from her pheromones that the Alpha was shocked by the sudden attack. Yet May gave in with everything she had—she had given Dove *everything*. Dove broke their lips apart when a moment of realization hit her, pulling back just enough for her to breathe against May's own lips. She closed her eyes as her mind clouded with thoughts.

"Is everything okay?" May's concern hit Dove square in the chest. This Alpha was not the one she knew. The woman in front of her was caring, sweet, and oh so concerned. She shut down her thoughts before scooching over in her bed for May to join her.

"Yes, I'm just ready to cuddle." Dove pat the center of her bed, coaxing the brightest smile from May, yet her self-doubt crept in. What if May didn't want to soothe her? What if it was the Alpha taking over?

"That's if you still want to join me?" She asked the question as innocently as she could, trying not to let her uncertainty creep in.

May didn't even hesitate before she crawled into bed, pulling up the thin blanket and the fur. Dove didn't usually sleep with fur before May spoke.

"Because you mentioned being cold." Realization hit Dove again. Even with the doors closed and the fire running, Dove was still cold. Would May notice when she was warm again? How had she not noticed how caring May was, or was this her heat talking? Either way, May's eyes held more compassion than anyone who had ever gazed upon her.

"I think sleeping would be good before the next round hits, not that I expect you to be here." Dove couldn't stand to look at May when she mentioned the last part. She rolled to her side, hoping that May would secure her arm around her waist. Before long May cuddled up behind her, and that limp cock she desired pressed right against her ass. She resisted moaning when May's arms lightly drew them together. It was everything to feel May's bare breasts against her back, and the deep breath hitting her neck. As much as she fantasized about her cock again, the body pressing against hers was more than enough.

"You asked me to spend the night, Dovely. I will be here when you wake up." May placed a final kiss to Dove's shoulder before they fell into a deep sleep.

***

Dove had no clue how long they had been asleep before the cramps hit her. She had started getting cramps around her waist during her last few heats. Someone had mentioned that it was an absence of pups in her womb, but all she cared about was how painful they were.

May's body was cradled away from her when Dove woke abruptly. She sat up, grasping at her waist and almost crying out from pain. Sweat dripped from her temples as the blanket fell away. Dove had to stand up and race towards her washroom as she felt the urge to empty her guts. She was on her knees over a bucket when a hand smoothed her back.

"Dovely, you are okay." May's hand grounded her back. They sat there for a few minutes before the heat kicked in again. Her vision turned into tiny white pinpoints while sweat erupted from every pore in her body. Each breath was a weight on her chest as May stood behind her, trying to soothe her. The only thing that would help her now though was May. No one but May.

"I won't be okay until I have you again." Each breath left her in pain from the lack of skin-to-skin contact with May. The Alpha rumbled above her as she scooped her up. She carried Dove bridal style before dropping her in bed. She bounced on the bed before May pounced on her, pinning both of Dove's hands above her head.

"Tell me how much you need me, Dove." May purred seductively.

The tight thumbs on her wrists compelled Dove to fight back. She pushed her bare breasts into May's naked chest, about to respond when her cramps threw a wrench in her plans. She doubled over in pain, clutching her empty womb as she pressed her fingers into each spot it ached. She needed to fill the pain with May's seed and a litter, no matter how illogical it was.

"I need your seed May!" When the pain lessened, she arched her breasts up again. "Pinch my nipples. Take me rough, May."

May growled above her, dipping down and taking one of her pink nipples in her mouth. She swirled, flicked, and bit just enough for pleasure.

"I love the freckles framing your beautiful breasts. I wish I could trace every one of them with my tongue." Her hot breath brushed against Dove's extra sensitive nipples. Vaguely, she felt a hand trailing down her stomach. "But you know what I want most, Omega?" The words were murmured in a low tone.

Dove bit her bottom lip, barely able to shake her head when May bit her taut bud. Broken whimpers burst from her lips when May's calloused hand stopped right above her pulsing clit.

"Answer me, Omega." May wasn't asking; she was demanding a response. Dove's Omega couldn't help but give in to the strong Alpha above her. She opened her eyes to see May lingering right above her.

"What would you like most, my Alpha?" Her voice was strained with ecstasy as May brushed her bundle of nerves for just a second.

"To lick every freckle on your pretty little pussy."

"Gods May, please do. Lick all of them." When she was younger, she tried to count her freckles, but they covered almost every inch of her skin. She never looked at the ones on her lower body, but now she wished she appreciated them more because of May's admiration.

"Especially this one right on your clit. It is so beautiful with the glistening slick your swollen lips produce. I will spread every drop of it over your beautiful clit." May's fingers applied a slight pressure to her clit, and Dove moaned as her body produced more slick. She couldn't stop it from dripping out of her core as May trailed and licked down her body.

"I dreamt about you like this once. What it would be like to taste you. To have you ride my face while your hands gripped my hair. Then I wanted to use all the slick you produced to slide my cock in you, while you screamed for my name. Begged for my seed."

Dove couldn't help but tremble when May licked up her slit. She wanted everything May spoke of. She desired May to take her fill of her pussy and then ride her cock until she cried for her seed.

"I want it. I want all of that." Dove was breathless from May's relentless lavishing. At one point she slurped all of Dove's slick as her fingers danced across her clit, her other hand grabbing one of Dove's breasts. While May kept up her attacks on her sensitive pussy, Dove reached down for May's curls to fulfill the other half of the wish. Her fingernails dug into the scalp of the Alpha's head while May pushed nearly every inch of her face into Dove. She let out a moan, which vibrated into all of Dove's body, setting her off. Her orgasm exploded from her body as May's tongue reached inside her pussy. She shook and trembled as May kept up her attacks. The Alpha moaned into her again, causing Dove's thighs to shake.

"May! I'm going to come again." Dove moved her feet, digging her heels into May's shoulder blades. May's tongue swept at Dove's cunt while she furiously played with Dove's clit. The stream of come she produced had barely stopped leaking out of her when her second orgasm hit. Her Omega cried out at the attack from the Alpha. Every nerve of her skin shuddered from the effects of her orgasm. She sank into the bed, unable to keep herself up. Dove felt her nipple being pulled and her clit being sucked, but it was too much.

She gently pushed May's head away, looking up at her. Her Alpha's face was covered in her wetness; blonde curls stuck to her forehead. May licked both her lips and put her fingers in her mouth.

"Your taste, Dovely. I can never get enough of it." Dove let out a gentle laugh before reaching towards May, almost begging to be held. The Alpha did not deny her request as she reached for the Omega.

"I don't think I can take your cock now." Dove gave a self-deprecating laugh. Her inner walls fluttered a little at the idea but the few waves of her heat were sated again.

"Ready for another rest period?"

"Hell yes." Dove didn't want to face away from May this time and crawled into her arms, burying her face into the Alpha's chest. May's oak smell penetrated her nose, and she let out a deep sigh before she slept. May whispered sweet nothings in her ear, ones that followed Dove into her dreams.

***

When Dove woke up in the morning, she had never been so relaxed. If she wasn't so in tune with her body, she would have thought her heat was over. She could feel small waves tingling in her as she got up and stretched. She flexed her toes, realizing the blanket had fallen off her body.

May was standing up with a chalice in her hand that held some type of juice. She had on the tunic she wore under her uniform. With the beige material hanging over May, Dove could think clearly.

The entire night had been more of an eye opener than she had ever experienced. May had been everything she coveted. Yes, she treated the Omega with all that her heat required, but when it came to her personal needs, Dove felt them meet. She had been just enough Alpha and dominant as she had been sweet, observant, and protective. There was no way that this was the May she knew. She had misjudged May their entire life, or at least the last ten years, and Dove had no idea why the caring, soft person in front of her would let her.

"I thought you would appreciate this; I went down to the kitchen a while ago and got you this and a plate of food." May brought the bowl of fruit and what looked like eggs to Dove, whose stomach was suddenly rumbling, yet she couldn't eat. Dove could only look deep into May's moss green eyes. They held so many emotions, but the bottom line in her pheromones was love. May loved Dove. She was undoubtedly sure as she watched May place the juice down and approach with worry.

"What is wrong?"

Dove sat up with the sheet clinging to her sweaty body. The Alpha's scent shifted to one of discomfort as she shuffled on her feet. May moved to kneel in front of the bed, tangling her hands in the blanket, but unable to reach for Dove's.

"I didn't mean to upset you, May. I just was never expecting to find myself here. With you holding breakfast after caring for me." The clouded judgment she held over the years seemed to affect her view on reality, when it came to May. Whatever Dove said seemed to affect May negatively. Dove tilted her head away from May. She didn't know how to fix the sadness that clouded the Alpha. Dove wanted to return to the moment before. Where she had May here, laying in her arms, and never wanting anything else. Dove tried using her pheromones to comfort her Alpha.

"I did not either." A few tears glistened in May's eyes. Dove didn't understand why May was so upset. Maybe May was remembering her true nature. An Alpha who wouldn't give into any Omega. May picked slowly at the sheets over Dove's body. "You did not need me, Dove. You have everything you need in you. I loved helping you through your heat, but you would have survived without me." She stood, anxiously playing with the blanket before facing away from the Omega.

"You're wrong, May. No one else could have satisfied me the way you did. I can't go back to the way it was before. I don't want to." She whispered the last bit, a silent question in her eyes. May must've understood her. She couldn't survive her heat without an Alpha, but it didn't have to be May. Now Dove was saying only May could, but the words didn't seem to process in the uneasy Alpha.

The thoughts of her and May avoiding paths while being around Taylor filled her mind. The two of them avoiding eye contact in the same room, and Dove pretending she couldn't smell the desire on May's pheromones. It would be torturous.

May turned to the side, grabbing her official coat. Dove wished May would sit down with her so they could talk about their issues. She knew she had been hard on May, but now looking at the tall blonde, she felt her heart break as May distanced herself.

"May—" She went to stand for May, getting ready to plead, but something stopped her.

"This is just your heat talking. We had a passionate night together and I satiated your heat. But you could not possibly want me, Dovely." May wrapped the coat around her arms, her scent now hidden from Dove. She tried to tap into the base instincts, but it was impossible. The barrier between the two of them that existed before was now present yet thicker than before. Dove had *never* felt this separated from May.

"May, *please.*"

May dropped her lips to Dove's forehead and handed her another fur. "I will send for some herbs for the..." It seemed she didn't know how to say it. Her seed?

But Dove could see it in May's eyes. What if Dove was already pregnant with May's pups?

She could imagine it. A little girl running around with hazel eyes and strawberry blonde hair. With her attitude and—

Dove stopped the train of thought. She couldn't go down that rabbit hole.

Maybe they should've seen this coming, but Dove didn't know how bad it would hurt for May to turn away from her naked form and go back to their lives. Unfortunately for Dove, she didn't know that May had only ever been in love with Dove.

Chapter 5

Dove was so frustrated. Of course, May would get up and leave her. Of course, Dove's pleas that they could be more would fall on empty ears. She knew who May was, so why did she think those soft whispers that had reassured her would mean May was a different person? She had seen the caring Alpha who helped her through her heat. She even found out that May hadn't had sex in over a year. But no, May wasn't any different. Dove saw a future of what they could be, but Dove would never be enough for May, and May would never change.

She lay on the bed as her mind ran through the night they shared together. Maybe it was all just primal need, yet she felt May. She got a glimpse of May's pheromones at certain moments. She felt *love*. Dove had thought May loved her when her defenses were lowered. Those pheromones had hit her like a brick just before her orgasms. The rest of their sex had Dove over the moon. Maybe it was just her heat though. Maybe she had imagined the love that lived in May's eyes and soul.

Tears filled her eyes. She was so stupid. It meant nothing. Just rutting and fucking in a heat.

When her tears finally dried, there was a soft knock on the door, startling her.

"Lady Fortenberry? The captain told me to bring you this. I will leave it at the door for you." She didn't recognize the voice, but the mention of May caused her frustration to rise again.

The fire had died while the slick had stuck to her legs. She felt dirty and went to the small washroom behind the wall. She would eat before she bathed herself, but she had to wipe off what was between her legs—the remnants of May's passion. Once she cleaned that off, she went to her wardrobe of clothes and grabbed the clothes that would hang loosely on her sensitive skin. The food sat right out by the hearth where May left it. She peeked out the door to see what it was and when her eyes locked on the herbs, she lost it all.

Fuck her.

Chapter 6

May realized just how much she fucked up when Taylor came back from her two weeks of passion with her new wife. She had seen Dove once or twice in the kitchen, but never around the royal grounds.

Usually, Taylor preferred Dove to help her with her daily meals. She wasn't Taylor's handmaiden, but she was definitely close with her. Taylor did not like referring to the staff as lesser just because they served the castle, which was something May valued. The morning when Taylor arrived at her office after two weeks away, she knew she had to be careful.

"You have got a glow to you." May set the paper down. Taylor rolled her eyes but couldn't hide the smile that accompanied it.

"Why don't you update me on what's been happening?" The Queen spoke with authority. In front of May was an informal request for one of her soldiers' reallocations with his mate being pregnant. The men had been married for many years, but May barely knew him. She would approve it regardless, as it reminded her of Dove and the throes of their passion just weeks ago.

Whaow Frar was at peace with all the neighboring countries and had a steady ruling, which was why the wedding had taken place. There had been concerns about the new tax for the people, but May wasn't worried about it.

May's official title was the Captain for the Queen's Army. She oversaw all the troops, which meant who was recruited along with lots of paperwork. Even with her unofficial political title, she knew everything that happened, and Taylor trusted her as her best friend. May gave her a quick and fairly boring rundown. The country had few city capitals and officials who were always in touch with the crown.

"I'd like to check in with the kitchen staff and thank them for their work. I also need to check in with Dove and see how she is after her heat." May nodded and kept her hand on her sword's hilt. Sometimes when her nerves hit, she would hold onto it to ground herself. The battlefield, the training, the feel of Dove.

"Have you seen her?" Taylor's concern didn't crack her voice, but it was evident in the way she spoke. Along with May, Taylor always had Dove's safety at the forefront of her mind.

"You know Dove does not like to be around me when you are not there." Taylor nodded, looking down at the parchments May presented her with.

"Of course, but you do so regardless. Anyways, let me catch up with these documents and then I'll go visit. I also would like to see the new recruits."

The recruiting period for the army didn't have a specific timeline, but it typically happened once or twice a year. The newest recruits were only a few weeks into training. It took almost half the year to make sure they were properly trained, if not longer. May took on two personal recruits, who she spent an extended period of time with to make sure they were the best. They would be generals, leaders, and maybe even a captain one day if May had her way.

"Understood. I have a training period marked out for the next two hours."

"Perfect, I'll swing by and grab you before our afternoon meal. Then we can eat with Dove." Taylor grabbed some of the documents and left the office.

May would have to go to the outside grounds where the recruits would be today. They had an indoor corridor for training, but with the pleasant weather, the recruits went outside for today. She had just chosen her personal recruits who were with the general guard today.

May got up, walking through the castle and acknowledging each of the guards under her command as she walked towards the gate which led to the training area. It was far from the garden and royal livestock but closer to the stables.

Her two most promising students were an Omega who was nineteen, and an Alpha approaching twenty-three, the oldest of the recruits. They were both excellent at following orders and fighting, but they sparked each other when they were together. Instead of realizing they were working on a team, they fought for May's approval.

The Omega, Kaden, was great at hand-to-hand combat but struggled using weapons, while Zoe the Alpha only used weapons. Today she wanted them to work on their weaknesses.

She was the captain, the first in her family. Her family grew up on the outer edges of the kingdom. They were shepherds, farmers, but when the war started, she was drafted at fifteen. She moved to the castle as a drafted soldier, and Taylor instantly took a liking to her. She worked her way up the ranks through the war, which led to her leadership position. Both her parents had grown older during the war, so she remained at the castle.

Her official position was sometimes too much. She did not like everyone waiting on her orders. She was growing tired of giving commands, yet she was only thirty. She had only been in this position for five years.

As May approached the stables, she saw about twenty recruits taking part in hand-to-hand combat. They all had fighting leathers on and sparring sticks. May thought it was one of the most ridiculous exercises, but if they were to be handed weapons one day, they had to be able to grasp the basics, with something less deadly. About five of the royal guards were overseeing the training along with her second-in-command, Caleb. He was drafted the same time as May, but he was about two years older. When she became Captain, she offered to relinquish him, but he refused to leave.

"How are they looking today?" She approached Caleb who gave a slight bow. Kaden and Zoe were on opposite ends of the field, and she bounced her eyes between them.

"They're all doing very well—except one of the younger Omegas." He pointed to the teenage boy who was frail. She could understand immediately, his technique was off.

"I would like you to give him some attention today, Caleb. I will be taking Kaden and Zoe for one-on-one training." Caleb nodded, walking over to the younger Omega and dismissing Kaden and Zoe. They approached her with reverence as May led them back to the office.

She brought her two recruits to her personal office, which contained a multitude of weapons and a sparing area, and took a seat at her desk.

"Today we are focusing on your weaknesses." May watched as fear flashed in their eyes. She thought of her own insecurities and fears. How she couldn't put Dove first. How she wasn't enough. She wasn't royal adjacent like Dove's family. She wasn't educated. All she was good at was fighting.

"Kaden, you will be solely working with weapons. No hand fights at all. Zoe, you will have a single dagger on you for safety, but I am not to see you use it unless it is an emergency. Same for you, Kaden. We will be going around with the Queen later, so be prepared. Until then, I want you to both continue what you were doing outside." They took their dismissal, but May sensed their hesitation. They exited through the wood door to a private sparring room.

Typically, she would watch and train them more personally, but today she had much to do. She pushed some papers aside, looking at the distribution of soldiers around the area. They were there for safety and at trade posts. The thing she hated most about her job was all the paperwork. Because of her lack of formal education, sometimes she felt she couldn't understand logistics. It was something her and Taylor had discussed earlier this year.

Before she knew it though, Taylor came knocking on her door. The two guards she always had assigned to her gave a slight bow.

"I will take it from here gentlemen but before you go, can you grab Kaden and Zoe and tell them to come here?" The older Beta nodded before running off.

While Taylor used the title Queen, she rarely wore dresses. Her royal suit was navy blue today, which offset her brown hair curled into a bun. She took a seat in the comfiest chair set in the corner, letting her legs fall apart and a big breath left her lips.

"Everything okay, Your Highness?" May addressed her formal title in case her trainees came in. They never used formality in private but today she would.

"Everything's fine, May. Just a long first day back." Taylor's behavior betrayed how she felt, though. Her breathing was labored. She was slightly pale, and her pheromones were brewing a storm of emotions. May was about to double down with her questions when Taylor spoke.

"As you know, we are waiting to try for pups, so I had to take some herbs, and it took a mini toll. Eveleen isn't in heat, but my rut started during our wedding period and we didn't want to take away from that bliss."

May and Taylor had previously talked at length about what it would be like to have pups and the perfect

situation. This was before Taylor met Eveleen, but May
knew how much she desired Dove. If Dove was pregnant
with her pup...She would do anything for Dovely, but
Dovely and her pup...May would cease to exist for them
if it meant happiness.

"Herbs during a rut are hard." Almost a year ago
May had experienced a rut caused by Dove's Omega. She
took no one and nothing but herbs and stayed in the
dark for almost a week until her rut was over. The whole
rut was one of the most painful things she had
experienced, and she had been stabbed during battle.

"Well do not stop there, May. Is there anything you
did to help it?" Taylor widened her legs, as to let her
length breathe through the pants. She would not
comment on her friend's length, but she saw it poking
through the pants and Taylor knew it. They were both
Alpha's after all.

"I avoided her. You know this, but every sniff of her
scent and taste of her pheromones drove me deeper into
the hole. As much as I wanted her, I knew that being
alone was better for both of us." Taylor nodded, resting
her hand on her lower abdomen. All May thought of
now was her Omega. Dove would look so pretty in the

kitchen corridor whether she was preparing food or washing dishes or baking food. Dove was always an effortless beauty.

"Basically, I have to rut Ev or suffer until we do?"

"Yes."

Taylor seemed disappointed at that answer, but she snapped back to life as May's two trainees entered the office. After giving formal bows to their Queen, they fell into line with May. The smell of their sweat from training burned May's overwhelmed nose. There was something underlying it, but May didn't question it.

"Kaden and Zoe, we will be following Queen Atwood around for the rest of her day. I hope your training session went well."

It was not a question on May's part but rather a statement to let her Queen know that these two were her trainees. Taylor gave the most subtle nod. Usually she greeted all the recruits, but May assumed the past two weeks had drawn all formal pleasantries out of her. Instead of addressing the two, she looked straight at May.

"Let us go to the kitchen first." May slipped into her typical captain attitude as she followed Taylor closely.

They walked through the corridor as May looked around, noticing all the small details. Most of her guards were forward facing and watching the Queen. The few staff that raced through the hall addressed her with a slight bow before they kept moving.

The walk towards the kitchen was a long one, which gave May time to think. How was she going to look Dove in the eyes when she knew what it felt like to have Dove's walls clutch around her cock? She could ignore the thought of Dove's naked body writhing under her, but she could never forget the feeling of Dove's pussy squeezing her cock. Now as they walked down the hall with her best friend, she had no clue how to address it. Her scent would give her away, probably as it was now.

"What is going on with you, May?" Taylor whispered while walking slightly closer to her friend.

"Your scent has been off all morning but now I'm walking next to a completely different person, so what is it?" The question Taylor presented her was more than enough to make her head spin. Why was she so weird? Sure, she was in love with Dove and helped her through her heat, but that meant nothing. Right?

Before May could form a response though, they had reached the entryway to the kitchen. Kaden and Zoe were standing by her sides as they entered. The fire and hearth used mainly for cooking was ablaze with multiple pieces of food—bread with sauce lay flat on the slab while meat from the livestock cooked over the fire.

All the staff in the small wooden kitchen bowed to the Queen who bowed in return. Taylor respected every single person who worked for her. Alpha, Beta, Omega, Staff, or Royal, it didn't matter.

"Welcome, Your Highness. We have various meals prepared for you and your staff. Was there anything in particular you would like?" Kelsee, the plump woman in front of her, was Dove's superior. May knew that Dove's father was a weapon's master and her mother was a housemaid to the royals. Dove had been raised in the kitchen due to her love of cooking. Her family was extremely close to the throne and would remain to be as long as it existed.

"Some bread would be excellent. If Dove is available, I would love for her to join us."

"Of course, Your Highness. Dove is with the livestock, but I shall request her presence. Please make yourself comfortable." Kelsee left in a hurry to retrieve Dove. May knew at this point that her heat was long gone. The only thing left between them was the memories.

Taylor rolled her eyes as Kelsee left the quarters, not because of her words or position but because Taylor continually wished she was treated as normal. She met May's eyes before questioning the most promising recruits.

"What did you two notice when we entered the space?" Taylor directed her question at May's trainees as she paced between the multiple pieces of kitchenware.

The left of the kitchen was where all the utensils were. The big wooden table stretched across most of the visible room as the hearth sat behind it. To the right was the larder where all the ingredients lived. A lot of their food was dried and stored there but most of the food was prepared fresh daily. It was the reason they had such a lively garden and livestock pen.

Kaden spoke up first. "There were multiple kitchen servants moving around the area. I counted at least eight. Five were Betas and the others were a mix. I suspected two Omegas and one Alpha." Taylor nodded along to the words before glancing at Zoe, who responded immediately.

"There are three exits. The one we came through, the one to the deeper kitchen and one outside to the animals. Kelsee took the one outside towards the animals. Two of the Betas retreated into the back almost immediately after we entered, but the cooks with knives remained focused on their task."

Taylor nodded along to each of their observations. May could not have said it better herself, stating the number of entrances and exits, along with the number of staff moving around the kitchen. On average, the kitchen staff had about twenty people working at all times, but there were about sixty on staff to serve both the royals, council members and staff.

"That was impressive from both of you, but if you were to join the guard, those observations must be firsthand." May instinctively gripped the sword attached to her hip while speaking to her recruits. They were both ahead of their class, but where one was lacking, the other was aware. She was about to point out the flaws in both of their observations when a lovely smell permeated her nose. While her resident sweet honey smell was still there, another scent was overpowering May's nose, an earthy one she couldn't quite place. May's Alpha flared to life, about to pounce across the room and demand who touched her Omega, when Taylor grabbed her wrist, stopping her.

Kelsee reentered the room, prompting both of her trainees to stand upright again. She had a small loaf of bread and Dove trailing behind her.

May couldn't stop the soft gasp escaping her lips when she saw Dove for the first time in two weeks. Sure, it wasn't a long time, but it had been two weeks since she was in her most intimate state with Dove. Her blue servant dress reached the floor, and her corset was barely visible, with beige linen covering Dove's toned arms. Her fiery hair was braided loosely, a few stray tendrils dancing in the wind, and with it her scent filled May's nose again.

Clenching her jaw so hard she thought her teeth would break, she lightly breathed the honey smell in. Dove smelled amazing, but it wasn't her usual smell. Her inner Alpha released a low growl in the room, which changed the atmosphere immediately.

Kelsee lowered her head, almost dropping the bread, while Zoe's Alpha came alive, almost ready to challenge May. She couldn't blame Zoe, who was just reacting to her nature. May was glad she had only given Zoe a small dagger, because she sensed the younger Alpha ready to launch into a fight over the redheaded Omega entering the room. Luckily, Taylor was able to step in.

"Thank you so much, Kelsee." Taylor pushed past the two Alphas on purpose to break up their standoff.

"Dove, I'd like to discuss things with you in private." Taylor grabbed her upper arm, which sent May's Alpha into a frenzy. She knew the relationship between her friends, and that Taylor was married, yet her possessive nature took root. She was the one there for Dove's heat. *Her!*

Before she could open her mouth and ruin everything, Taylor cut her off. "Thank you, Kaden and Zoe. You both show promise. I'll meet up with you later, Captain." It was a dismissal if May had ever heard one.

Chapter 7

The last two weeks for Dove had been horrible. The rest of her heat was excruciating and the only thing that comforted her was the thought of May holding her during her orgasms.

The days after May left her, Dove couldn't stop crying. All she wanted was May, her arms around Dove with soothing words being whispered in her ear. Instead, all she heard were her own tears.

She had curled up into a ball on day two, refusing to eat anything brought to her. Kelsee had prepared her favorites, but the thought of eating made her sick.

By day three, she was just angry. She couldn't even think about May without wanting to punch one of her walls. No thoughts could soothe her fury at the Alpha. The one who promised to give everything she needed and then bailed when Dove tried to get serious.

By day four, she realized her mistake. She could barely process any of it. While most Omegas were in tune with their bodies, Dove had her days when she didn't know herself, so when she felt her body change the smallest bit, she realized she had forgotten to take the herbs May had sent her.

In her blind rage she decided not to take them, and now she may have a pup in her belly. Some would say it was too soon to tell, but Dove knew it. She could feel the life—or lives—inside of her growing. The ones her and May made together.

"How are you, Dove?" Taylor's piercing gaze read right through Dove. "I know May helped you through your heat, but—"

"I don't want to discuss May, Taylor. Everything that happened was in the past. I would rather talk about your honeymoon." Dove spoke with a slight eyebrow wiggle. A blush colored Taylor's cheeks at the mention of Eveleen. She had been that way ever since the two met over three years ago.

"Eveleen is perfect as per usual. She is slowly getting into her role as Queen." Eveleen grew up in a small village far north of the palace name Jaeredale. She had come to the Queen after her mother passed, and they had met months before. Taylor was instantly drawn to the Omega when they met and refused to take anyone else as her Queen.

"That is a very formal response, Your Highness. I was more interested in the physical aspect of your honeymoon." Dove led her to the back of the spacious place where all ingredients were kept.

The royal kitchen had multiple larders and pantries for various items. Dove had been in the livestock pen gathering fresh eggs and milk for a meal she was preparing to make when she was summoned. Her father had been out of the castle for a few weeks, and he was coming home soon.

While she didn't live with her parents anymore, she still ate weekly meals with her family. She didn't live in the designated servants' corridor that most of the palace staff lived in. Instead, Dove had her own room located in a nice wing that was close to Taylor. She served her duty to the throne, earning her spot, but sometimes she did soak up the perks of being close friends with the Queen.

Dove spent most of her evenings on the balcony overlooking the garden, watching the animals who played at the edge of the forest. At least, when she wasn't reading.

"Eveleen wanted to try using a few explicit items, which was definitely a smart idea from my wife. We barely left the sheets. Is that what you wanted?" Taylor stopped when Dove grabbed some of the supplies she needed for her recipe. She had grabbed two eggs and a pail of milk before pouring it into a jug for safe storage.

"That is exactly what I wanted." Grabbing her ingredients, she marked them up for personal use and for not the palace staff. She placed them in the cooling area, feeling Taylor's eyes on her. Dove never kept anything from Taylor, and assuming how May reacted to her coming in from outside, she could only assume Taylor was smart enough to piece together their current tension after her heat. Letting out one deep sigh, she turned to her friend.

"I can feel your desire for questions, but I refuse to talk about it here. If you want me to discuss it, you'll need to stop by my room later tonight."

Taylor pursed her lips, but Dove could read her like a book. Before Taylor could speak again, her head of staff entered.

"Your Highness, there are a few officials looking to speak to you." Taylor glanced back at Dove before giving her a slight nod, following him out the door. Her scent made it clear that this conversation wasn't over.

Dove's official job was gathering ingredients and food throughout the day. She wasn't head or keeper of the livestock, but she made sure that everything went according to plan and what they produced would be suitable for everyone the kitchen fed. Sometimes she focused on the garden, which had their own servants. She was also responsible for making food for the army staff a few times a week, but all the main cooks shuffled around who they cooked for to keep things entertaining.

She went through her day, prepping what she usually did and making sure everything was up to quality. Kelsee came and checked on her before sunset, making sure she had everything set up for the next day and dismissing her.

"Dove. Before you go, I noticed you haven't been enjoying your usual meals. Was there anything going on that I need to be concerned about?" Kelsee had always looked after Dove like a second daughter, but sometimes she went a bit far. Right now, she was over being the fragile Omega.

"I am all right, Kelsee. If there were any problems with the kitchen, I would let you know. I must be going, though. I have a meeting with the Queen." Dove went to exit the room, carrying a small knapsack of food she could properly dice up in her room and cook. While most living quarters didn't have a kitchen, Dove's had a small area to prepare meals and a hearth where she could cook meat.

Dove walked the corridors of her home. The old stone that was built a few hundred years ago crumpled in some places, but the floors under her feet remained as well constructed as the first day. Guards were placed evenly apart to make sure everyone was safe. They all greeted her with a simple nod.

The kingdom she lived in wasn't too populated, unlike outside countries. The castle itself housed less than a hundred and fifty people on staff, excluding the army. They all knew each other fairly well, and while Dove typically never left the safety of the castle grounds, she had a community here.

She continued her journey to her quarters while her mind raced. What was Taylor going to ask her? Had May said anything about their night together, or maybe Taylor had just pieced it together. She hadn't been able to look May in the eye earlier. Maybe that gave her away.

As she neared her room, her thoughts became too overwhelming. Taylor was her best friend; she could be honest with her. They had grown up together and Dove could barely remember a day apart from Taylor. She pushed her door open, finally breathing easier for the first time since seeing May.

After cooking up some potatoes and lamb, Dove gathered her book and made her way to the balcony. The spring air filled her nose. Even this late in the evening she could smell the dew from the grass below. The sky was a mix of orange, violet, and pink, small clouds floating in the upper atmosphere as she watched.

Her mind started conjuring up images. If she had a pup soon, would she sit here at night with her little pup in her lap? With the pup lazily looking up at the stars while she curled the soft hairs around her fingers? A tear slid down her cheek at the thought. She had always wanted a family, but she never expected it like this.

Would May accept her and the pup with open arms, stepping up, or would she be angry and want nothing to do with them?

Dove couldn't fathom the thought of finding out she was pregnant and having May hate her. She had made this decision for them, whether it resulted in pups or not, she felt like she owed it to May to tell her. And whether Dove wanted to admit it or not, even as anger clouded her judgment, she wanted May in her life. Much like Taylor, she couldn't remember a day without her since she turned fourteen.

Dove had always been frustrated with May. Taylor was an Alpha but because they were so close she never felt their natural roles dominating their relationship. When May made captain, she noticed the Alpha more. The one who commanded people while not taking the Omegas around her into consideration. During her heat, she realized that was what drove her to hate May. It was what she did, not who she was.

She set the leatherbound book aside when a small knock filled her ears.

"Dove, may I come in?" Taylor's voice filled the silence in her room. But before she could stand up, the

Queen entered her room, dressed in a soft colored tunic that reached past her knees. This was the side of the Queen no one was allowed to see. Dove hadn't seen this her side of Taylor in a while.

Both of Taylor's parents had died during the war. Her mother when she was thirteen and her father at sixteen. Her mother had been poisoned, sending the king into a blind rage that got him killed in battle. While Taylor had spent her whole life being raised for this role, she had been only nineteen when she was crowned.

Since Dove's parents had been secondhand to the Royal family, and Taylor was her best friend, they adopted her into the family, metaphorically. Whenever Taylor needed a motherly figure or hard advice from a father, Dove's parents were there. Taylor was more like a sister to Dove than a best friend, and it would always be that way. She was able to comfort Dove in a way others could never achieve.

"Did May hurt you in any way?" Taylor's first concern was always her safety. May and Taylor had always treated her like a delicate little flower. Sometimes she thought it was fair since she barely left the castle, and they had seen war, but tonight she wasn't in the mood. The pheromones that ran through her revealed her frustration. She didn't need protection! All these emotions had been cooking inside her for weeks.

"Everything that happened between May and I was consensual." She slammed her book on the bed before padding into the kitchen to clean the mess. Taylor's own pheromones that were meant to soothe Dove pushed her further into rage. She didn't need any Alphas to comfort her, not even her best friend.

"Are you sure it wasn't your heat?" She drew closer to Dove, gathering the utensil and placing them where they could be cleaned. Dove practically ripped them out of her hand to scrub them with the water she had.

"Sure, my heat may have clouded my judgment and chosen the closest Alpha, but I don't think I could have survived it without May. No matter how mad I am at her. She was sweet, but then she got up and left me as soon as she got her release." That wasn't the entire truth. She didn't need to tell Taylor about their passionate and intimate night together and how May hadn't left her until Dove threw pressure her way.

"I think May—"

"No Taylor, do not speak for her!" Dove faced her friend, almost yelling. She hadn't even noticed that tears were streaming down her face. Two weeks of emotions finally broke free. "We had sex but at one point it felt..."

Taylor's brown eyes held worry when Dove collapsed into her arms. Taylor held her friend as she cried furiously. They sat on her fur rug, Taylor's scent creating what felt like a safety blanket. As they sat, Taylor ran her hand up and down Dove's back, telling her it was okay. After a few minutes, Dove finally gathered the courage to speak again.

"It felt like she was making love to me. I got a glimpse into what she was feeling, or what I thought and then she left me there. Alone." With a sniffle she pulled back as Taylor tucked a stray strand behind her ear.

"We let our guard down during our heats and ruts. She could've been revealing how she felt for you without realizing." Taylor spoke as if she knew what May really thought, but Dove refused to tap into it.

"I know I've been hard on May and over the years I've spent a lot of time complaining about her, but this was a side of May I hadn't seen. At least not since we were younger." She pushed off Taylor's body, moving towards her bed. The fur felt good against her feet before she collapsed on her soft bed. "It was the May I used to know when we were teenagers. The one who would cradle me while we kissed in her bed. The one who promised me every time she left for war that she would come back to me. That's who helped me. The Alpha who broke my heart."

"I know how you feel about May, Dove. You don't have to explain, but I also know that May isn't all that you think she is. You know I love you, and I love her but after that one incident May asked me not to interfere anymore." The incident in question was about five years ago when Dove was in heat and May had been super sensitive towards her. Her heightened emotions made her upset because she had had a brief argument with May earlier about a woman. This was a few years after the abrupt ending of their teenage relationship. From that moment on she had stayed away from May and was aggravated at everything she did. Now she was wrong.

"It must be hard being friends with both of us." Sniffling, Dove pulled at the furs on her bed. She had washed the thin sheets on her bed after their passionate night, but she couldn't get the smell of May out of her room. Off of her.

"It is hard sometimes." The Queen padded towards her, grabbing the water chalice Dove had poured for herself earlier. "But I know things from both of you." She arched an eyebrow at the same time gesturing to her belly. "I understand why you are upset and maybe that led to some...illogical thinking, but communication is the key to any relationship. Eveleen taught me that."

She dropped to eye level in front of her friend. "I don't know what is going to happen, but I think I know how you feel or want to feel, so talk to her." Handing off the chalice, she watched as Dove downed the rest of the water. She heard what Taylor was saying.

"I have to go now, Eveleen is a snuggler."

Taylor patted both of Dove's knees and gave her a tender kiss on the top of her head. "By the way, if you and May have pups together, they'll be the sweetest pups I know."

Chapter 8

It had been six weeks since Dove's heat, and May had been avoiding her more than usual since that day in the kitchen. When May was around her, she noticed subtle changes in Dove's attitude. Her scent was completely different to what May was used to, but was so alluring to May. She wanted to bury her nose into Dove's mating gland, soaking it up. If she did that though, she would have to mark her. She wouldn't be able to resist being that close to Dove again and not sinking her teeth into the supple pulsing flesh. She could barely remember the way it tasted when she ran her tongue along it.

She continued hands-on training with Kaden and Zoe while getting swamped with daily paperwork. The outside territories were requesting more troops due to civil unrest. People were infuriated with the higher taxing laws yet there weren't enough soldiers she could spare. After the civil war, most were relinquished back to their homes. May could understand going home, but she also needed to protect her people and land.

May sat at her desk as her body began stiffening. Ever since she helped Dove through her heat, she had been on edge. She could feel her rut trying to burst through at any moment. This morning, she witnessed Dove dressed in a royal green outfit to attend to the throne. May could not remember the reason, but she knew that the green with Dove's fire hair set a spark in her.

Her cock had instantly hardened at the sight. The dark green gown had complimented the Omega's skin tone. May's cock grew a heartbeat of its own after seeing her and smelling that sweet scent. Even now almost an hour later it continued beating as she sat at her office. Dove's hair had grown significantly longer. It usually took a while, but the red tendrils sprouted the past few weeks, growing past her shoulders.

May had been left alone with her paperwork for the past half hour or so. There was no one around that could stop her. The bulge in her uniform grew larger with each moment. May blew out a deep breath as she gripped her cock over her uniform. She threw her head back, releasing a groan. She had to grip the side of her chair to redirect her energy. The gold iris of Dove's eyes filled her mind. She pinched the tip of her cock through the fabric. Dove's freckles came to mind. The ones that lined her shoulders and neck as bright as the night sky.

She rubbed up and down the length of her uniform, the pressure driving her insane. Releasing the buckle that held her uniform together, she sprung to life. Pre-come lined the tip of her cock so May used it to slick the length. She gripped the head, her most sensitive part, and pictured Dove down there, her rosy lips wrapping around the head of her cock. She would probably make a snarky remark before taking May as deep as she could.

May's head hit the back of her chair as she continued her pumping. No one had sucked her cock in almost three years. If she were to feel Dove's mouth on her, she would burst immediately.

The image of Dove swallowing her seed was what made her unravel. A bit of her come sprayed over her hand and onto her uniform. May had to fight from releasing an almost painful groan. While she would usually never think of Dove in a sexual situation, she couldn't stop the rut in her body. She had already felt Dove's body wrapped in one intimate sense, she could barely imagine the other. That soft tongue that molded to hers would apply fierce pressure to her length. May could hardly imagine it without her cock releasing another burst of her come.

After letting her body deflate, she looked down at her uniform, which was now soiled. There was no way she could clean this up in her office. After tucking herself back in her clothes, she let her head drop to the desk.

May sat there for a few moments, before gathering one of her sweat rags to wipe off what she could. Her rut was going to destroy her this time around.

There was only so much she could handle, and today she needed to leave the castle. Grabbing her protective wear for the outside, she wrapped herself up before escaping to her own room. May didn't even acknowledge her guards as she made her way to her private corridors.

Once she entered, she threw her soiled clothes down before making her way to the wardrobe in her braies. Before she could fully pull them off, a knock sounded at her door.

"May? It's Taylor, I'm coming in." The door opened when May was fully naked. Taylor didn't even bat an eye, probably sensing her oncoming rut. They had compared sizes plenty of times, but May was sometimes sensitive about it during her rutting week.

"Was there something you needed from me?" May pulled on her off-duty uniform. It was more of a protective corset, trousers, and a cape that blocked the view of her sword.

"If I were able to read your mind, I would be able to tell you wanted to leave the palace grounds." Taylor hooked her hands behind her back. She had her royal blues on, currently more present as the Queen than her best friend. May couldn't acknowledge that part of her friend right now.

"I am going out. I will be taking Kaden and Zoe for some training." She had her sword and belt secured tightly around her waist, but her light blonde curls still needed to be tied into a bun. She reached around her back to try and pull it up, fumbling with the loose strands.

"Let me help you May." Taylor moved behind her, carefully pulling her hair up and tying it loosely into a bun. May appreciated the care her friend put into the simple action.

"I think it'll be a good idea to clear your head. Eveleen has been talking about going out into town. She wanted to get some things." When May realized what her friend was hinting at, she turned to Taylor.

"I would be happy to take Your Highness into town. I will get a few more guards to come with us." May walked to her nightstand to grab her pouch of coins and secure it tightly to her waist. She didn't have a lot of money on hand, but what she did have she kept it under lock and key.

"That would be lovely." Hesitation rolled off Taylor.

"Was there something else?"

"Dove would also like to go." At the sound of her name, a small rumble left May's lips. How dare she so casually throw out Dove's name like she was just another Omega. Taylor continued.

"You know she never asks to leave the grounds, so I would really appreciate it if you took both of them." Taylor must have sensed May's Alpha trying to start a fight. The other Alpha backed down, throwing her hands up with a little surrender. May knew she had nothing to be jealous of when it came to her friend, but she could only reason so much.

May never acted like this outright aggressive where Dove was concerned, but ever since their night together, she couldn't help it. She had caught Dove's scent even if they weren't together, and it drove her to her naturally possessive nature. Dove may not have been her Omega, but May was Dove's Alpha.

"Gladly. I will gather up the guard. Can you gather Eveleen and Dove? We will meet them at the gate."

Taylor gave her a swift nod before adding her gratitude. She went back to her office, gathering both her trainees and a few extra protective details for the Queen. On her way to the gate, she gave instructions to both her trainees.

"Today we will be riding into the town square with the Queen and Dove. Neither of the Omegas have any training in self-defense and are highly respected in our kingdom. You have both demonstrated every quality I want to see in recruits, but you are both still lacking in your weaknesses. Today we are going to continue focusing on those, just like last time."

Nervousness rolled off both her trainees. They quickly tried to cover it up but with her heightened senses from the upcoming rut, she caught it.

"This is both of you putting your skills to the test for the first time outside the castle. I understand the fear, but if I did not think you were ready to defend our Royal Highness, I would leave you here." They both said nothing as May spoke.

She stopped walking and turned to her trainees. Zoe was muted in her subtle grays, but Kaden sparkled in her black gear. The tension between the two was still as evident as ever.

"If either of you think you are unfit, this is your time to back out. I will not judge you as this is protection for our Queen, but you must say so now if you feel unready." The trainees looked between themselves and gave a proper nod to their Captain. May valued both of them and their dedication. She trusted that they would bow out if needed, and she took that to heart as they kept walking.

"All right. With that in mind, once again, Kaden—you will only be using weapons. And Zoe, only your fists. If needed, you will have access to both. There has been some tension in the city, so I do not expect complete peace on this journey. Keep that in mind."

They neared the gate where the carriage would be ready for Eveleen and Dove. The thought of sitting on a saddle for half an hour almost drove May insane, but she had to be out with her guards.

The smell hit her before May's eyes caught her. It was even more prominent than this morning. Her eyes darted around until she caught sight of Dove. She had changed out of her formal attire to a leisure dress that was perfect for the springtime. It was a pale yellow that wouldn't normally go with Dove's skin tone, but she looked like an angel. Her hair went from a loose braid to waves being let down with a tiny bit pulled up at the top.

May couldn't help herself. She marched right up to Dove and searched her eyes. She *had* changed, but May just couldn't figure out why.

May inhaled deeply, closing her eyes as a mix of her pheromones and scent hit her nose. Her honey smell was on blast, as if a breeze had been put directly behind her to stream into May's airway. It was *everything*. May wanted to gather Dove up in her arms and give her all the kisses in the world. She resisted pulling Dove against her, but her entire body protested, begging for the Omega.

"Hi. Thank you for taking us to the Reverwallow market." Dove's breath was airy. Her words danced carefully around May's ears, as if testing the waters. They hadn't had a single conversation in six weeks. It was no wonder she spoke slowly. May's eyes narrowed on her, taking one final inhale before backing up.

It might seem unprofessional to everyone else around, but with Dove near her, no one else existed. The only other Alpha around them was Zoe, who glanced cautiously between the two. May almost growled at her, but Zoe shifted her eyes downwards. No one else caught their silent conversation. It was a battle of pheromones and even though they were more civilized, they couldn't help their nature.

Realizing her mistake, May gave a slight bow to her Queen, Eveleen, whose light brown skin shimmered in the sunlight, her dark spring curls tied up with a little bow. May had deeply admired the Omega for her best friend. Eveleen was the perfect amount of gentleness needed to combat Taylor's hardened demeanor. Over the years, and every interaction with Eveleen, she had grown to love her.

"Your Highness. These are my two trainees, Kaden and Zoe. They will be accompanying us if that pleases you?" Eveleen grew up on the outskirts of the country, similar to May. She was not used to any formalities, even though she now had the official title of Queen.

"They seem lovely. I would just like to pick out a few things for a project. Taylor wishes she could be here, but I am glad to get away for a bit." She shared a smirk with Dove. The two Omegas were close friends. They were both known in the castle and loved by everyone. They were known to always be cared for, but the way Eveleen looked at Dove forced May to let out a low displeased rumble. Caleb took over for her.

"We should get a move on so we can be there before lunch." He helped the two Omegas safely into the carriage while May made sure both horses were secured. She would be riding by the side of the carriage to make sure it was protected from all angles. Eventually, the group left, and May suffered in silence as her horse trotted slowly. When she wanted to escape the confines of the castle, she never imagined being stuck by the woman of her desire, especially this close to her rut. She decided it was best to stay as far away as possible from Dove.

May would never claim to be the smartest in a room, but she was smart enough to stay away from Dove today. Even though she was in a carriage, May could sense Dove's scent. The honey smell infiltrated every one of her senses. The relaxed pheromones from being with a friend hung in the air. May almost sighed at the peace radiating from Dove. She closed her eyes, but her mind couldn't stop conjuring up images—tasting Dove again with her new honey scent, the slick that would coat her face when she made Dove moan her name. Dove under her as she released her seed into her waiting womb.

Her eyes popped open at that thought. She already felt what it was like to come into Dove. What if the knot that kept them together formed a pup one day? Dove would look amazing with her pup, her smell on Dove's body. Would her pup have fiery hair or her light blonde locks? She sighed before galloping closer to Caleb.

"Since we are close, I am going to go ahead and check the perimeter. Kaden and Zoe, stay here." Closing her eyes, she shook off all her thoughts as a few tears escaped her eyes. May forgot whatever reality she conjured up.

Chapter 9

Dove was having an excellent time as they walked down the road. She had her evening meal with Taylor and Eveleen in their private quarters the night before, where she had mentioned wanting to go into the town square to find a few specialized ingredients to make something up for her own birthday. The main ingredients were Crimson Currants and Fuyote, a vegetable from the eastern region of their country.

Along the road were buildings where the townspeople resided, small drinking taverns, and places to get food. The road was kicking up dirt as they walked closer along the small city towards the town hall. They had sectioned off a place where locals of all status could sell their stuff, and each merchant tent was spread out in the little market.

Dove and Eveleen went to each stand, lingering at the ones selling cloths since Eveleen had mentioned wanting some fabrics to sew her own blanket. It was something Eveleen did with her mother before her passing and now she was teaching Taylor.

The guards were close enough to protect, but far enough away to not be able to hear their conversation. Dove's eyes wandered occasionally to May, whose scent was radiating with anxiety. Dove felt the overwhelming urge to comfort her, when Eveleen interrupted her thoughts. Even though they hadn't talked and she was still angry at May, she hated seeing her uneasy.

"What do you think of these?" Eveleen questioned, raising a small light blue cloth with a daisy pattern.

Dove traced her fingers across the fabric. It was almost as soft as one of her favorite blankets. She leaned in, smelling that the soft square was scented.

"It's perfect for a small pup, wouldn't you agree? The name could be sewn right below the flower." Dove gave Eveleen a sideways glance, making sure May was out of earshot. She was, thankfully, busy talking with Kaden who was viewing a few small daggers.

How the Alpha hadn't picked up on her pregnancy she didn't know, but she was just glad she hadn't. When May had marched up to her earlier, Dove thought she would throw her over her shoulder and take her somewhere private. Instead, she just stood there, smelling the change in her pheromones. The change...their pups created.

She would tell her soon.

A few days ago, Taylor had confronted her, telling her the smell was distinct now and other Alphas would be aware. That any Alpha who tried to get too close would have the pup's scent flooding their system. Taylor had mostly told her this out of concern and set up a doctor's appointment for her. She practically pleaded with Dove to tell May. She suspected Eveleen knew but she tried her best to mask it. It was her life anyway. The pups—or pup—were only the size of a bean.

"It is very pretty. Maybe one day you and Taylor's pups could be swaddled in it." Dove turned to walk to the next stand, where a lovely old Omega was selling different types of jewelry. Dove ran her fingers along one of the rings. Something about it caught her eye. She traced her fingers along the silver band.

"That's gorgeous." Warmth spread through her entire body when the Alpha stood by her side. Instinctively, she leaned back to rest her head against

May's chest. She knew her hormones were driving her, but she couldn't resist the feel of May behind her. Her body heat radiated nicely against the windy town. A small gasp broke from May's lips, causing Dove to straighten her spine. Dove resisted looking at her and continued walking towards her desired goal.

"It's outside my budget. I still need to find my ingredients," she muttered. Padding along the town's path, she finally found who she was looking for.

"I need a few Crimson Currants and a Fuyote." Dove told the merchant. Eveleen rejoined her side while the merchant went to find the fruits and vegetables she needed.

"So, what is this dish you are making?" Eveleen's questioned, scanning the wide variety of fruits in front of them. They ranged from villages all over the country.

"It is a type of noodle dumpling. The Fuyote is put inside the dough along with some cabbage and chives. It is cooked for long hours in a slow oil that isn't the standard one we use in the kitchen." She picked up and inspected some other greens she may use in her meal.

"What are the currants used for?" Eveleen picked up a few berries that she knew were Taylor's preferred sweet snack. Eveleen really was the most attentive Omega Dove had met.

When Eveleen arrived after the death of her mother, Dove and May discovered that Taylor had been in communication with her for months. It was clear their friend fell faster than they could have imagined.

"It's used to make a drizzle and a marinade for the lamb that goes with it. It's incredibly sweet and it pairs perfectly with the meat in my opinion. When I started cooking with my mother, she taught me that recipe, but I found the Fuyote on my own."

"I can't believe your twenty-ninth birthday is in a few days!" Before Dove could respond, the ingredients she was in search for were presented to her.

"They look exquisite! Thank you." Dove happily clutched the bag to her chest, handing her coins towards the excited merchant. She turned to look for her guards. May wasn't anywhere to be seen, but her two recruits were. Zoe was closer to her and would barely make eye contact with her. Her duty remained to Eveleen, but the way she stood close to Dove made her believe she was doing it for May's benefit. She started approaching the younger Alpha when a loud noise rang out in the square.

An unruly Beta was making a scene at one of the vendors when his eyes caught on Eveleen.

"This is your fault." The dark-haired man stepped closer to her and Eveleen, aggressively pointing his finger while swinging the bottle in his hand. "It's your wife who has upped our taxes and ruined my business." He stopped just short of Eveleen, before Kaden stepped in with her hands on her sword. Eveleen's pheromones were more distraught than Dove had ever witnessed. She was a non-confrontational Omega, and this Beta was threatening her.

"Sir, I need to ask you to step away please." Kaden set out her other arm to block Eveleen, but Dove remained entirely open. Zoe was nearing her side, but it was too late when the Beta lunged at Eveleen, who was pulled away by Kaden, leaving Dove wide open to be tackled to the ground.

Dove couldn't process the world around her as the air was pushed out of her lungs. The Beta landed on her in an awkward angle, his glass bottle falling at her side. The commotion around her was too much, so she shut her eyes. This is why Taylor and May never wanted her out of the palace. When she left bad things always happened, and what if this time it resulted in the loss of her pups?

She felt the pressure of his body leaving her when Caleb hauled him up, putting him in restraints. Zoe crouched beside her, carefully cradling the back of her head. The Alpha's eyes were flush with concern, but the only thing she wanted was May holding her while she cried. She always responded poorly to physical pain, and she already had heightened emotions.

"Are you okay? Is the pup?" Zoe inspected her body with her eyes checking for any signs of bleeding. She spoke the words so casually as if Dove being pregnant wasn't unusual. The young Alpha had picked up on it, which was even crazier that May hadn't. May had always been a bit aloof with some things.

Dove cradled her belly, waiting for the faint thump of the heartbeat. It had barely started beating a few days ago, but when she tuned in, she could feel her pups growing in her. A low growl caught Dove's attention as a dark figure broke through the crowd.

"What the fuck is happening here?" The words came out of May's lips so fast it was unrecognizable, before she descended next to Dove's body. If she wasn't so distracted, she might have shoved Zoe off of Dove. Instead, Zoe stood up to work on crowd control and the world faded outside of May.

"Dovely what happened? Are you all right, baby?" Her Alpha pheromones were the most comforting thing Dove felt in weeks; she couldn't help but surrender. Her body melted when May cradled her head, carefully pulling her up into her lap. May soothed back some of the red hairs that were stuck to her face. Dove held it together as best as she could while letting her Alpha calm her. "I have got you, Dovely."

***

The rest of their trip was a blur, while the other guard members gathered up the carriage and horses. May refused to leave Dove's side through it all, taking her time to "evaluate her trainees" as she claimed. Eveleen was on the other side of May with her own guard. The Beta that attacked Dove had been taken to the local prison with the local guards.

Kaden and Zoe moved with efficiency to get the horses together. When it was ready to go, May finally left

Dove's side before reassuring her she would be right back. Eveleen approached her instead.

"I think I'll ride on horseback on the way home."

"Eveleen no, definitely not. You were almost attacked."

"Yes and because of that you are hurt. The only people on the way back to the palace are peaceful farmers. I want to do this. You and May can ride in the carriage together." Eveleen's eyes were pleading with Dove as she spoke.

"Taylor will kill both of us if something happens." Her Omega felt the instant urge to touch her belly where her pups lay. She glanced up at her Alpha double checking the reins and rubbed her belly for a moment.

"Then I'll tell her I ordered you guys in there. Maybe you can finally talk."

"There's nothing to discuss." Eveleen dropped her eyes to where Dove rubbed her belly, prompting her to drop them. She stepped closer to her friend, lightly touching her wrist.

"You were assaulted and hurt. What if something happened to the pups because the guard's main concern was me? I would never forgive myself."

"Pups? What pups?" Just like that, the Alpha she had been desiring for weeks found out the news she was deciding to tell her later tonight.

Chapter 10

To say the ride back was awkward was an understatement on Dove's part. May refused to ride in the carriage with her even after Eveleen ordered her. If it was a serious matter, she could have been charged with treason for disobeying a direct order. Instead, Eveleen let it go, and they rode back in silence. She apologized multiple times to Dove who sat silently on the ride back. All she could think about was the look on May's face. Nothing had ever hurt Dove more.

May's face was painted with fury and anguish. If she wasn't so attuned with May's pheromones, she would have assumed May was overcome with anger, but instead she was experiencing an overwhelming sadness. A sense of betrayal. She had never seen or felt May so distraught. It caused a physical pain in her chest, constricting her every breath. Dove's Omega whined. All she wanted was May's smile back. The smile that lit up her heart. Instead, she saw a tear running down May's face as she mounted her horse and went ahead for a perimeter check.

She hadn't seen her for the rest of the ride. Dove never felt so guilty. The pups growing in her were a result of May and her. When they got back to the palace, Taylor rushed to her and Eveleen's side, bringing them to the medical wing.

"Tell me everything. No details spared." Taylor stood next to Eveleen, holding her hand while the doctor examined the back of Dove's head along with the pups. Eveleen launched into telling her wife what happened. Taylor rumbled at one point, placing a soft chaste kiss on her wife's lips. Taylor noticed she hesitated near the end.

"What else is it? Is it the reason you're so distraught, Dove?" She glanced between the pair of Omegas, running her hand up and down Eveleen's arm. Dove, who had been previously glancing into Eveleen's eyes, looked away. She wasn't angry with Eveleen; she was angry at herself. She was the one who caused the pain on May's face. *Her.*

"Dove I am so sorry I—"

"You did nothing wrong. You were right to express your concern, I just wish she hadn't found out that way.

Her Alpha was crying when she found out." Taylor's audible gasp broke through the silence.

"She knows?"

"She knows." If Eveleen wasn't rooted to her side, Taylor might've dashed out to check on May. It was who she was. A loyal friend, always concerned with her family.

"Have you talked to her?" Taylor moved closer to Dove. The presence of her best friend provided little comfort. What she needed now was her Alpha. The sire of her pups.

"I was going to, when I was ushered to the medical wing by my Queen." She bumped her shoulder with Taylor's. She loved Taylor but she wished she was less protective right now.

"As soon as we get the guarantee that my nieces or nephews are okay then you can talk to her." She bumped back. "But I also think maybe she might need more than a few hours to process."

"I understand but—"

"This is out of left field for her. You knotted, she thought you took the herbs, but instead you didn't, and you haven't discussed anything since then. May would never suspect that you are pregnant, and knowing May, she is taking every emotion she has at one hundred and ten percent Dove, especially because—" She cut herself off to look at Eveleen.

"Especially what?" Dove gripped her best friend's hand, dragging her gaze back to her.

"It seems my wife isn't the only one who's horrible at keeping secrets. Granted, I've kept this one for almost ten years," Taylor whispered, then laughed when Eveleen's lips turned upward in a sweet smile.

"Taylor?"

"May has been in love with you for years." Dove's mouth instantly went dry. The words rang through her ears. She thought through every interaction she had with May over the last few years. All were blinded by her frustration with the Alpha but if she tried to look past it, she could see the small caring gestures May had in all their engagements. She had missed it all along. The way May would make sure she was safe, well-fed, and happy. She always made sure Dove was happy, even though Dove held nothing but annoyance for the Alpha. She didn't deserve her. Especially not to mother her pups.

"I must go talk to her." Dove stood up, clutching her belly. The pups in her were the closest link she had to May right now.

"Hold on a second. The doctor hasn't even let us know if the pups are okay." Eveleen, the voice of reason, stepped in to grab Dove's other wrist so she didn't leave the room.

"They feel fine." Both Queens had a questioning expression as she headed for the door. The doctor stepped in with papers and a vial of what she assumed was medicine.

"Miss Dove?" He glanced at the three pairs of eyes watching him as he flexed the parchment between his hands. "It seems that you and the pup are okay. With the head damage, I did want to provide you some medicine for any potential pain. It will not harm the pup at all. I would also like to see you again in two weeks to check on the pup." She tried to ignore the singular use of the word pup and focused on the good news.

"That sounds like an excellent plan, doctor. I'll make sure Dove is here for that checkup. In the meantime, we will retire to our rooms." Taylor shook the doctor's hand before ushering them out of the room.

As she walked the corridor, Dove thought of everything she would say, but Taylor spoke first. "The only thing May wants is true validation. She has never once thought she was enough for you and definitely not now with a pup. Dove, explain your choices. I still don't know how you feel about having her as your co-parent, but that little part of her DNA is growing inside you, so you have to discuss your feelings."

Taylor left her in front of May's door. She had never been so nervous to knock in her life. The May behind the door wouldn't be her Alpha anyways. She would most likely be angry, demanding things of Dove. Either way, she wasn't ready for whatever version answered the door.

***

The last few hours of May's life were the most horrifying. She had killed people on a battlefield, lost multiple friends, and many events in between, but nothing made her feel as horrible as finding out the woman she loved was pregnant with her pups and refused to tell her.

Once May had heard the words outside the carriage, her brain pieced everything together. The exquisite smell coming from Dove, the acceleration in her rut, the extreme possessiveness she felt for the Omega.

She sat further down in her chair, swirling the bottle of whiskey she had. Her legs were wide open as the fire crackled in her ears. May's limbs were tingling with the alcohol in her system, but it was barely enough to dull the mental pain. She was unable to stop herself from replaying the memory from earlier in her mind.

Every single bone in her body felt crushed with the weight of the truth. She wasn't enough. She would never be enough for the woman she loved. She had never felt this *awful.*

May felt like every breath was choking her. It wasn't air she was breathing, but poison. It didn't help that the words kept ringing in her ears. Like a funeral bell tolling.

Pregnant.

Dove was pregnant with her pups. Dove didn't even respect her enough to tell her. To care about how she would feel to tell her Alpha.

She took another swig of her drink, swallowing down the burn when a knock sounded on her door. She knew immediately who it was. She could smell the initial honey and now the overwhelming scent of the pups filled her nose. Those were hers. The pups' smell was used to warn Alpha and Omegas alike.

She could barely move from the chair when Dove pushed the door open, to which May almost cried at the sight. She was a radiant beam of light.

"May?"

"What, Dove?" She swirled the whiskey bottle in her hand again, before almost downing the rest of her bottle. The Omega entered her space, still dressed in the same outfit as before, some dirt lining her dress.

"How much have you had to drink?"

"Does it matter? It is not like I am pregnant." She slurred her words, but they still halted Dove in her tracks. It was a low blow, but it was all she had right now to keep from breaking her heart anymore.

"Maybe not, but I assume you don't want to feel bad in the morning." Dove squatted in front of her, trying to draw the bottle out of May's hands. May gripped it even harder, dragging the bottle to her lips. Chugging more than a few gulps, she kept eye contact with Dove, whose

Omega was clearly displeased at the action. Her lower lip trembled.

"Did that make you feel a bit better?" Dove asked when May finally relinquished the bottle to her. Dove placed it on the ground, still settled in front of May who could barely focus on the Omega's golden irises.

"Are you pregnant?" May could barely force out the word as she kicked her feet to the side. Even though Dove's dress was caked in dirt, she was as gorgeous as ever.

"May I—" She cut herself off, gripping May's hands to bring her attention back to Dove. May's Alpha broke at the sight of the pretty Omega in front of her. The tension between them was so thick it could be sliced with a knife. So much hurt and distrust flowed between them. May knew Dove wasn't entirely at fault for the lack of communication. Yet to find out such an important piece of information through someone else ate away at her. Was she truly so low on Dove's radar that she never felt the need to be included in this decision? May would carve her heart out if Dove asked, but right now it was shattered.

"You are pregnant. With a pup. You always wanted a pup. I am just sorry it is mine." She wanted another swig of her whiskey. Dove never trusted her! Once she pieced it all together, she felt stupid. So stupid. Obviously the reason Dove smelled better was because her scent was all over her.

"Don't say that, May. Please don't ever say that again." Dove moved, pulling May to stand with her. She slowly guided them to May's soft bed, who lay sideways as Dove set her down. All she wanted was to shove Dove away, curl up, and cry, but every piece of Dove was meant to draw her in. Her pheromones, her scent, her beauty. May was hopeless.

"You clearly do not think I am ready either. But how am I supposed to traipse around every day knowing you are holding my pups? Knowing one day soon you will have my pups, and I will not be there because you do not trust me." May would cherish her pups. As soon as she discovered that Dove was carrying her pups, she knew every responsibility was second to her family. Nothing was more important than her family, no matter how unconventional it was. But she was still angry. May loved Dove. She wanted to be her mate, have a life with her, to love her with every inch of her soul, but she didn't want Dove to feel the same out of spite. Her pups would be brought into the world regardless of the parents' relationship, but looking at Dove standing in front of her, she fought every urge to break down and cry. The Omega, the woman she loved, didn't love her in the slightest.

"We'll figure this out, May. I promise. I was planning on telling you soon, but I figured you would piece it together before. I know that isn't an excuse, but I am so sorry you had to hear it from someone else." Dove stripped off the first layer of her clothes to not get May's bed all grimy. Her undershirt and undergarments were still covering her body. She lay on her side, facing May.

"Why did you not take the herbs? I sent them to you." May lightly brushed the orange strands out of her face. There were tiny grains of dirt in them. Dove's content sigh lifted a bit of sadness off May's chest. Just enough that she felt she could breathe.

"I was so angry at you for leaving me. When we were together, I got a glimpse of how you truly felt and then you just left." Dove's hand went to her belly. "It was dumb and by the time I realized it had been days later. I didn't want to take them and hurt the pup accidentally, even if I wasn't pregnant."

May moved as close as she could without touching her fully. She rested her forehead on Dove's collarbone. She smelled like May, bringing a small smile to the Alpha's face.

"You could feel what I felt?" She pressed a tiny kiss to her skin. There was little to no resistance left as she lay in bed with Dove again.

"Your pheromones were giving you away when you were in me. This overwhelming sense of happiness, relaxation, and love. It made my heat so much better. I thought maybe it was just the moment, but afterwards when you were caring for me, it was so much clearer." She kissed May's head. "Then when we separated, I had a realization that I felt that way too, outside my heat...I spent all my time analyzing us, May. You have always been the kindest soul to me. I've been so naive."

"Do not talk down about yourself, I will not hear it." Slurring her words, May snuggled closer into Dove's warmth, a deep sigh fighting its way from her chest.

"I know I've spent years hating you but that was my own heartache. I thought you were engaged with other women, and I was jealous. I wanted you to want me and only me, but May I want to raise our child together. I want to be with you. I want to stop denying myself." Dove whispered her words, afraid that it'd break any bit of progress they had made. She could finally admit how she felt, why she hated the Alpha, but she didn't want that reason to push May further away.

"I want that too, but I think we need to have an honest conversation first." Lazily, May threw her arm over Dove's waist, pulling her in closer. "I am still upset but I want to try, just not when I am so sleepy." The Omega's hands played with the ends of May's golden locks.

"Why don't we just lie here? We can discuss the rest tomorrow." Dove pulled the blanket over them while May surrendered to the warmth of her Omega. She knew that she would remain frustrated with Dove and herself for a while, and that they had work to do, but while May lay there in Dove's arms, she slept peacefully for the first time in weeks.

Chapter 11

Dove knew she had messed up and she swore with every bone in her body she would fix what she almost broke. The morning after they woke up together in each other's arms was peaceful, for about ten minutes. May started getting sick as soon as they wiggled out of the bed. Dove spent a few minutes holding back her hair as she emptied the previous night's drink. She massaged the base of her neck, trying to use her pheromones to comfort the sick Alpha.

The sickness didn't last long and then it seemed like the reality of yesterday hit May. Once May had gotten dressed in her leisure uniform, she turned to Dove, who noticed how the air had changed. May was standoffish with both of her hands tucked into her pockets, retreating to her washroom once again.

Dove could tell May wouldn't be the first to approach this time. Now was time for her to step up.

May had always been there for Dove, even now, so now Dove would be there.

"What happens now, May?" She wanted to believe that last night was more than blind hope, but right now with the Alpha withdrawing from her, Dove had no idea what to think. Even with May always giving Dove space that she needed, she never fled from her.

"I think I need a bit of space to come to terms with this. You have had weeks to process this, but it has been less than a day, Dove. I just need to think." May wouldn't look into her eyes as she spoke. Dove's shoulders sank with each word, but it was only fair. Like she had said to herself multiple times, Dove decided this for both of them.

"I understand. Whenever you're ready, May. I'll be here." She left to her own quarters to get dressed for the day, her thoughts drifting back to last night.

Even though May was drunk and upset last night, she had responded perfectly. She said everything Dove needed to hear, which was much more than she deserved. She spent most of the night awake with May in her arms. She had to resist grabbing May too tightly. Ever since the night of her heat, all she wanted was for

May to hold her, but the situation ended up reversed. The soft, warmhearted and kind Alpha was in her arms, all of her emotions written on her face as they spoke. May slept soundly curled up around Dove, a little grumble here and there, but everything in her body remained serene, at least until dawn when she woke up sick to her stomach.

Dove went through her day nervously, which turned into a week of nervousness. She didn't think May was actively avoiding her, especially because of the rumors of civil unrest due to the new tax laws—May was currently busy. Dove knew that May had struggles with the procedural and political side of being Captain of the army. May had never spoken to her personally about it, but she had been active in multiple conversations between her, Taylor, and May.

Dove felt terrible for adding more stress to May's political duty, along with training recruits. In the second week of May avoiding her, she was starting to feel the side effects of having a pup.

Her mornings were filled with throwing up. Her diet was starting to change and her body always felt bloated. With the stress of May finding out about the pup, she had avoided her birthday meal. Dove had all the ingredients set aside but they were starting to go bad.

It was late into the week when she decided to cook up the dumplings and meat she had wanted weeks ago. Dove had spent the week almost glued to Taylor's assigned staff. She knew that Taylor had ordered the switch and refused to speak out about it, but until she and May talked, she would be grumpy about it.

Dove passed the last half of the day making sure the dough for her dumplings was correct, folding the Fuyote and other vegetables into the breaded cocoon. All eight of the dumplings were sat in a thin film of oil before she would cook them later tonight. She ground up all her Crimson Currant berries, mixing it with a sweet gelatin. Grabbing the lamb chop she had set aside, Dove stirred it in with the fine red paste. She would let it sit for a few hours before baking it tonight.

"Her Royal Highness is in the front room." One of her fellow kitchen staff spoke behind her.

"Which one? Taylor?" The others practically gasped at the Queen's name being thrown around so liberally. She rolled her eyes; they all knew about their relationship.

"No, Highness Eveleen." Dove wiped her hands off in the wash bin and then slipped off her apron that covered her brown dress for the day. She trusted no one would mess with her food as she walked away.

When she rounded the corner to the front of the kitchen, Eveleen stood there with something in her hand.

"Would you be willing to walk with me?" Eveleen didn't wait for her, instead walking towards the main gate that would take them outside. Her two guards shielded her, closer than usual.

"Is everything all right, Eveleen?" She started to hustle to catch up to her. Eveleen didn't slow down for a single moment before they reached fresh air.

"Of course." Once outside they relaxed into a stroll towards the garden. Dove noticed Eveleen holding something before the queen spoke again. "Taylor told me I should wait until closer to the due date, but I was too excited." Eveleen presented a small blanket with multi-colored fabrics. Each square had a different pattern or design, but they all meshed well together. The small baby blue cloth with the flower was in the middle.

Dove started to tear up lifting the blanket to her nose. It was so soft and made with love. A few tears fell from her eyes. She understood that she was pregnant and would have a pup, but the blanket made it so much more real. To feel something physical that her pup would be swaddled in. Something her and May would use to wrap the pup up safely from the world was one of the best feelings. She rubbed her belly. After the slight confirmation from her doctor a few weeks ago, whether it was one pup or multiple, she would have all the love in the world for them.

"This is an amazing present, Eveleen. What happens if we have multiple pups though?" She attempted a joke when Eveleen drew her into a hug.

"That just means I need to make more blankets. I know Taylor and I are waiting but I'll be so excited to have little ones running around." She gathered Dove's elbow so they would stroll together. She could sense a bit of hesitation from the Omega next to her but kept an open mind.

"Have you been talking with May?"

Dove knew that in the future, communication was going to be an integral part of her relationship, so she remained receptive.

"May has been avoiding me. It hurts a bit, but I understand. I've kept her at arm's length for years and now one night together has created a link between us that will never go away, and it's all because of my decision." Eveleen bit her lip and nodded along to her words.

"Have you tried reaching out to her?" Eveleen stopped to crouch down and touch the flowers. White petals and yellow centers danced in the wind. Eveleen cradled one with her hand before releasing it. The way the Omega Queen radiated such softness took Dove's breath away. She was so graceful, and Dove wished she had that.

"I want to, but she asked for space. I spend every night and morning waiting for her to show up saying she's ready to talk, but I can't approach her. I have to respect her for now."

"You are meeting with the doctor soon, right?" There were plants all around them as they walked through the garden. To their left were the flowers which had been growing for just a few years. Taylor had decided to decorate the grounds with flowers for all the fallen army members and lost civilians after the war. The food that was growing was lined up to the right. A few of the palace kitchen staff were attending to it, looking like they were trying not to overhear their conversation.

"I have an appointment in a few weeks. My mother has been all over me since I officially told them last week. They keep questioning me on who the Alpha is, but I won't be telling them till May and I talk. My father was angry." Eveleen bit her lips. She clearly knew something, but Dove held her lips. Eveleen stopped to face her and drew her into another hug.

"I best get back to Taylor. May will come around, and when she does, you can present your child's first blanket." With a kiss on the cheek, she bowed out of the conversation with her two guards, leaving Dove alone in the garden. She looked up at the sky to see the sun close to setting. She went back to the kitchen to gather her ingredients, preparing to cook in her room.

Chapter 12

The smell of Dove's dumplings infiltrated May's nose before she could even knock. May's hand shook unsteadily at the door with the other gripped the end of her hair. Tonight she was hoping they could lay down most of the groundwork between the two of them, but she had no clue how it was going to go. Building up her emotional wall, she knocked. She knew that being honest and open with Dove was the best way to approach this, yet her mostly broken heart told her not to. May was at odds with herself since she never held herself back from Dove.

"Dovely? May I enter?" It wasn't long before Dove whipped the door open, almost slamming it on her own face. Her hair was paired into two braids with a flower in the left one. Dove had changed into a comfortable pair of clothes that hung loosely off her body. From what May had asked the doctor, most of the physical changes would take place in another ten weeks or so. The uneasiness shown on Dove's face could be read in her pheromones. May's first instinct was to soothe Dove's worry.

"Please come in, if you'd like to. I was just making my birthday meal even though it was two weeks ago. I've been hoping you would stop by and—" She leaned in to cut off Dove's rumbling. May couldn't stop herself. Her first and only love was standing there carrying her pups. She had avoided her for as much as she could the past few weeks to get everything ready, or so she hoped.

The feel of Dove's lips on hers left her walls crumbling. If she didn't back away, she would have pulled Dove up into her body and made love to every inch of her. May ended up pulling away, grabbing Dove so she could rest their foreheads together. They weren't okay, not even close, but she really hoped tonight was the start.

"I have missed you so much, Dovely." She pressed a small kiss to the side of Dove's forehead before entering the room and making herself comfortable. Dove's uneasiness was still evident, but it was replaced by a surge of joy.

"I..." Dove quite literally was speechless when May sat at the one of the chairs in front of the fire. The smell of her Crimson Currant lamb cooking was delicious to May. She wasn't sure what she was going to say. She knew what she had spent the last two weeks doing and thinking, but as she sat near Dove, all her thoughts disappeared. Luckily, Dove stepped in.

"I am almost finished with my lamb, the dumplings are being cooked in the pot, but would you like some water?" The Dove in front of her was hesitant and uncertain as she placed one hand on the underside of her belly. May's Alpha swelled with pride when she thought of her pup—or pups—growing in the Omega's belly.

"Water would be nice, but I would like to talk first." May tried to comfort Dove with her scent, but she was only able to do so much. She was nervous all on her own, without thinking about Dove's reaction to her idea of their future. Dove fell into the chair across from May with concern flashing on her face. Her freckles were blushed as she pushed one of her braids aside, tempting May with the scent gland on her neck.

"Can you just tell me if you are going to be here or not? I understand if you don't want to provide for me and the pup. And that what you said the other night was under the influence of whiskey but if you've changed your mind, I understand." Dove was rubbing her belly as she spoke with almost no faith in May. Now she remembered why she kept her distance and what the topics they needed to discuss were.

With everything in May, she flicked her green eyes up to meet the Omega's golden orbs.

"I will provide for you and the pups every step of the way, but I want to communicate about what our future will look like and decide things *together* from now on." She sat both her hands in her lap to stop herself from reaching out to Dove. "I have talked to Taylor about some things, and she insists we need to talk, that there is a lot we do not know. I had to take a few weeks to get some stuff into place, Dove, but I am ready to talk about this. Our pups and our future."

May could barely see the gold lining Dove's irises with the tears blurring in them, but she could tell they were tears of happiness. She knew Dove wanted to lurch out, bury her head into May's neck and pepper her with kisses, yet they were both still reserved, and they needed to be.

"I'm so glad you feel that way. I want you to tell me everything you feel and need from me."

"No Dove, it will not work that way. I will tell you what I feel and need, but you have to do the same for me. You are not allowed to hold anything back from me anymore, Dovely. You are carrying our pups and I need you to speak to me honestly. If you cannot promise me that then..." She trailed off. She would be a part of her pups' lives no matter what, but if Dove still wouldn't speak openly after everything, then May wouldn't be able to give her heart to her. She had done it long enough and now she needed to protect her family in whatever form it came in.

Dove stood, moving towards May. She gripped both May's hands before getting on her knees. The only feeling she could sense from Dove was an overwhelming sense of happiness. There was nothing else below the surface as May looked into the eyes she loved. The ones who provided a surge of joy whenever she saw them.

"You're the only person on the planet who calls me Dovely." She ran her small thumbs over May's knuckles. "My parents don't even call me that anymore. They stopped calling me that when I expressed how much I disliked it, but when you call me that, I melt. The name reverberates through every inch of my body. It makes me...*warm*. There was never a point in knowing you that I wanted you to stop calling me that, especially now. So, I promise you, May. I will tell you everything, starting with this." She gripped tightly on May's left hand, bringing it to her lips. "I promise, no more secrets."

May gathered Dove up, drawing her atop her lap. Even if they weren't going to be in an intimate romantic relationship, she had to have Dove on her. Dove happily complied, almost crawling into May's lap. Wrapping her muscled arms around Dove's waist, she squeezed her against her own body. Dove sat almost perpendicular to her, but just like always, it was a fit. She took a deep breath of Dove's scent. Her sweet honey was slowly being joined by an almost earthy smell. May was unable to identify it precisely, but she smiled against her Omega's head.

***

The sun had set since May had come to Dove's room. Her Alpha was slowly taking small bites of the lamb Dove spent so long making. May seemed happy with the food Dove had been dreaming about for weeks. A small purr built in her chest when May let out a moan of happiness. The Alpha looked up, raising a sandy eyebrow.

"You enjoy the lamb?"

"It is very delicious, Dovely." She cut it into one more slice, bringing it to her mouth. They had finished the dumplings a while ago also, which prompted May to let out an almost orgasmic moan. One Dove would never forget. Dove loved cooking and sharing it with people but sharing her food with May was different.

After sitting in May's lap for way too long, she got up and checked the food. She loved the feeling of being wrapped in May's arms. It was a safe space after spending all these weeks in a state of uncertainty. But the silence was getting a bit uncomfortable as she read more into May's body language. While they had had a bit more conversation about communication, they hadn't actually said anything about how they would raise the pup, or if they would be together. Dove wanted to wake up every morning with May lying next to her.

"You mentioned talking to Taylor about things. Was there anything in particular?" She didn't know how to advance this conversation, but maybe their best friend's name would invoke something. May immediately stopped her chewing and set the food aside. The self-conscious May she had started to recognize rose to the surface. She had seen it during her heat, during their conversation with whiskey, and over more than ten years of acquaintanceship.

"I have been discussing with Taylor for a bigger place for us. Somewhere with room for pups." May spoke quietly, almost daring Dove to be upset when the only thing she felt was love. May always thought about her first, and now she was thinking about their child first.

"I know you may not want to move and I understand that. If you do not want to live together, I also understand, but I thought if we had a big enough living space for us and the pups, it would be better. If you do not agree, we can keep our living quarters separate." May's worry seeped into the room, basically becoming its own person.

"May—" Dove's voice must have not properly conveyed what she was feeling because May stood up to pace the small confines of her room. Of course, May would have noticed that neither of their quarters would be suitable for both them and even one pup. While most Alphas and Omegas had two or three pups, Dove knew they would have only one.

"I should have asked you before even talking to Taylor, but I know she knew you were pregnant and since this is her castle, I thought it would be okay." May was standing near Dove's balcony, which had the doors open. The breeze blew May's scent and uneasiness into the room.

"May, look at me please." The dark green eyes found hers. May was worrying her bottom lip. Dove needed to show her how much she loved the idea. She put her own food aside before standing and grabbing May's hand. When May was gathered up in Dove's arms, her toes on the rug, she finally caught her attention.

"I would love to move in with you, because that is what you're asking, right?"

Dove gazed up at her Alpha. May glanced down at her, bringing her nose to Dove's ear. She breathed in a few times before whispering a warm *yes* into Dove's red hair. She locked their bodies together as if they were going to dance.

"If we live together, though, there are certain things that must come with it. I will need a bit of a kitchen workspace like this." Dove pointed to the area, as if May hadn't seen it a dozen times. She spun them in a little circle, pointing to the little table she had near the head of her bed. "This table must come with us." Spinning them again, she motioned to a few other items in the room, pointing out things that wouldn't drastically alter whatever May's plan was. She knew May had her own things and they would have to decide where each item would go. She didn't know the space of the new quarters, but she trusted her Alpha and best friend.

"The quarter is between both our current rooms but up a floor and closer to the royal wing. I know you prefer to live closer to the kitchen, but Dovely, this is our family, and I want us to have as much space as we need." She held Dove closer, pressing their chests together. She knew May was beaming with the thought of her pups and Omega this close to her.

"If I have to live and sleep without you for another day I might claw my hair out, May." Dove dropped her chin just below May's collarbone to look up at her. She had presented the idea of them being together multiple times, and May had dismissed it each time. Since their last chat where Taylor insisted May had been in love with Dove, she had overanalyzed every interaction she could remember.

"That was the next part of what I wanted to discuss."

"So, discuss?"

"I think the day I met you, Dove, was the moment I realized how much I could be attracted to someone. As we grew up there was never anyone else, Omega and Beta alike, that could compare to who you are. I gave up sex a few years ago because there was only one person I wanted. You." May's green eyes gazed into her own. Dove had lost count of how many times she cried tonight but this one might be the most impactful. The Alpha she thought who just went around fucking random women was professing her love.

"There was no one who made me come alive except you, Dove. There still is not. Now that I know how you feel, there is no one else for me. I will never go back to another person when I love you and you are here. So even if you do not want to be with me, I am here because

I exist for you." Dove halted their movements. She already had May holding her close, but it wasn't enough. She needed to be in her arms. She hopped up, prompting May to grab her bottom with both hands, holding them both up.

"May, I can't remember the moment I realized I was yours and how much you loved me, but since then I have spent every moment trying to earn you and be worthy to carry your pup."

"Our pups," May growled, hauling Dove closer.

"Our pup. I want to be with you and share every experience with you, if you'll have me."

"Oh Dovely, I have been waiting to have you for years."

Chapter 13

The next few weeks passed with many difficulties, but tender and soft moments filled those gaps. With the tension growing in nearby towns, May had to figure out how to divide her soldiers. Caleb had been helping her but the pressure of strengthening and nurturing her relationship with Dove while making sure the kingdom was safe was getting to her.

They slept apart for the first few days, trying to get their schedules in sync but after almost a week apart, Dove begged May to sleep next to her during the night. May was unsure if it was the pregnancy hormones but a few of Dove's tears had spilled over when she pleaded with May.

Taylor had gladly accepted them both wanting to move their quarters, but it took a while to get everything together to move. Because of that, May spent most of her evenings in the Omega's bed, holding her until they both fell asleep. They made small talk, and May would rub her belly and kiss her neck. It was one of the few times she felt completely at peace. No thoughts, no stress, just calm as she held her Omega.

Even though they both decided that they wanted to be in a relationship, with all the chaos they had only exchanged a few kisses and one heated make out. May could tell in the last week that the hormones were starting to affect Dove, causing her to feel bloated and self-conscious. Now that she was in the fourteenth week of her pregnancy, her belly was starting to swell with their pup. Every time May saw Dove, her Alpha brimmed with pride. She did that and Dove radiated with their pups.

Today would be the first night they would spend together in their own quarters. May had spent all day waiting till she could go home. Tonight, they would sleep together in their new bed. It was a huge moment in May's life, and she was counting every second till she could say she officially lived with Dove. Even though the past few weeks had been rocky, this felt like their first step towards their new life together. Like it was finally real.

"If we bring the soldiers from Sutherland to Atesa, we can have them evenly dispersed between both of the cities and the castle."

May barely paid attention, unable to even remember the numbers of each soldier in each region. She gripped her forehead and took a deep breath, looking at the map of her country.

"Yeah, I think that is good." The political sense of the job got more overwhelming with each second. Her guards were to protect every citizen from every civil disruption, and she was expected to oversee it all. She sat back in her chair and sighed.

"I will go ahead and talk about this with Taylor." She folded up all the paperwork, but Caleb didn't leave.

"I know you are overwhelmed with this and your family, but I'm here to help. We've been in this together from the start, May." May knew that. She trusted Caleb with her life. There were so many moments when he protected her and helped guide her, especially as an older Beta. If there was someone in the army, she had to choose to replace her, it would be Caleb.

"I understand. As of now, there is still stability, and I cannot think about anything else. Thank you, Caleb." He nodded along to her words before giving a sympathetic smile and leaving.

She had no idea how to handle this stress with the new pups coming. They still had many months before the pup or pups would even arrive, but she had to make sure everything was going well with Dove, and that she was safe and protected. She didn't expect any retaliation in the castle for the raised taxes, but she would let nothing harm her Omega and the mother of her children.

Before May even had a moment to breathe, Taylor entered her office without a knock.

"There was an incident earlier this morning. A lot of people are upset because they think these higher taxes are now being used to compensate for the wedding. I need to hold a meeting with the council and the town's political leaders to explain the decision." The rest of Taylor's ramble went on deaf ears.

She couldn't keep doing this, juggling politics and training with the pregnancy. Under her anxiety was excitement, but she couldn't even enjoy it because of her stress. She wanted to wake up every morning feeling excited for her new life. But recently, she found herself waking up most mornings in worry.

"May, are you listening?"

"Yes of course. Do you have a date for this?"

"In about a week or two." She nodded along but once again drifted away.

"You are worried about living in new quarters," Taylor guessed.

"Not able to escape to my own space when we have a fight is stressful," May joked, running her fingers through her curls. Since she wasn't training today, she had left her mess of a hair down. The curls were so naturally tight, but the colder months are when they started getting extra springy. She gave Taylor a self-deprecating smile. The only fights they would have would be from May not providing enough, but she would do everything for her family.

"Have you two been fighting?" Taylor leaned over her desk, concern written all over her face. She hadn't been talking to her best friend as much as she should, but she knew how Dove was. Dove had invited her to their weekly dinners but May had been too busy to join. She also refused to impose on Dove and Taylor's personal time. May and Taylor had their own time together, even though most of it was work related.

"No, I am just worried." Taylor rubbed her hand in what May assumed was supposed to be a comforting gesture. "I do not know how to do this, Taylor. How to properly live with Dove and provide what she needs. She has been telling me I am doing everything right these past few weeks, but I feel she is just trying to soothe me." She set her head on the desk. They had been working on their communication daily, but May still just didn't trust herself. How could she be enough for Dove, who was perfect? When Taylor spoke, May rolled her head to the side to look her in the eyes, head still on the desk.

"I've told you communication is best. I trust that Dove would tell you what she needs, but May, you need to believe in yourself." Taylor stared deep into her eyes when she spoke. "You have always stepped up and protected Dove and that isn't going to stop now. You will mess up, but you are the most loyal and caring person I've ever met. You just need to believe that."

May was unable to respond as Taylor stood in front of her. Her friend was an excellent leader. She cared for every citizen under her command and felt she was an equal herself. Hearing the words from Taylor soothed just a bit of her.

"Why don't you take the rest of the day? Make sure your quarters are settled before Dove gets home." Taylor gave her a little wink before leaving her office. Having a few hours off sounded just like what she needed, and her Queen was approving it.

Grabbing her personal items, she blushed at the thought of her and Dove breaking in their new bed. Having sex again for the second time excited her Alpha. Suddenly the thoughts of claiming Dove in their new room prompted her to leave her office. May hadn't been in the bigger quarters for about three days.

She raced through the hallways of the castle, trying to keep her composure. Everyone would be able to smell her excitement as she rushed forward, holding her cape closely to her body. She almost instinctively went to her old quarters before she remembered.

May opened the door, drinking in how all of her and Dove's belongings filled the space. To the right was their four-poster bed, with the collection of Dove's furs and a few of May's thin wool blankets. There were two wardrobes, one on the right side of the bed and one lining the wall. Their balcony was almost a direct path from the front door, with their hearth on the left end of the room and the little kitchen area for cooking. Their washroom was located behind the living area that was adjacent to their table from May's room. It was May's ideal home. The little newborn pups would be to the left of their bed, closest to Dove. She started tearing up, before placing her cape on the hook of the wardrobe.

All her worries went out of the room when she could suddenly imagine their whole life in these quarters. Dove would feed their pups by the fire at night before they would crawl into bed. The little pups would learn to crawl on the soft furs, leaving out small wooden toys that May would probably trip over. When they got older, they would move into the quarters next to theirs. The space next door was currently occupied with their extra stuff but would eventually be for their children. May's Alpha cried at the thoughts, ready to see the pups in their space, their home. They still had a bit to go, but she would spend every second preparing.

After making sure almost everything was in place, May collapsed on their bed and accidentally drifted into a little nap.

The sound of the door clicking open woke May. She jumped up from the bed, getting into a defensive position, but her shoulders relaxed when Dove walked in, carrying a few vegetables in her knapsack. May noticed that Dove had been focusing on food for her pregnancy to make sure the pups were well-nourished. May rushed to her side to grab Dove's food. Her scent was overwhelming, filled with...happiness? Uneasiness? May couldn't put her finger on it.

"This place—" Just like May, she teared up. Maybe she hated it and May messed up, but when she first introduced her to the space, Dove had practically hopped into her arms with excitement. Now May was unsure. She resisted from crowding Dove but used her scent for comfort. Placing her hand on Dove's wrist, she brought her hand up to kiss it.

"What is wrong?" Dove's gaze fell to her, and May could finally read through it. It *was* happiness.

"It's everything I dreamed of May." Dove grabbed May's unoccupied hand and spun in a circle. Pure elated joy radiated from her face, setting off a light in May's heart. She urged May to drop the food before doing a small tour of their quarters.

"A room like this with the table and the little kitchen set up." Dove took it in like a young pup getting a present. She then led them across to the open doorway. "A balcony with our chairs where we can look at the stars." Dove did a little hop. "Oh, and the mountains over there!" She brought them back in, leading towards the bed.

"A bed for the two of us." Dove continued while gathering close to May, who was beaming at the sight of her happy Omega. Dove threaded her hands in the curly golden locks before capturing May's lips in a kiss that lasted just a second. She rubbed their noses together before pressing her head to May's shoulder.

"A bed for us where we will fall asleep together every night. Where we will lie with our pups and read them stories. Where we can make love." Dove pulled back to look up into May's eyes. Her Alpha was overwhelmed with pride. *She* had brought joy to Dove's face. "It is the perfect place for us, May, and you thought of all of it."

May leaned down and kissed her pregnant Omega. The love of her life stood in front of her, flooding the room with her joyous pheromones while she grew their pups. May couldn't stop the happy tears that grew in her eyes.

"This is everything." Dove pulled back even though May wished they were still kissing. "I love you, May."

May's heart stuttered to a stop. She never could have imagined this moment. She remembered the moment she knew she was in love with Dove and spent every daydreaming of her since, but she never could have seen this coming. She almost didn't believe it, but the grip at the back of her neck told her it was real. Dove loved her and her heart swelled.

"I love you too, Dovely." They kissed again before May dropped to her knees, kissing her Omega's belly. "And I love you too," May whispered to her pups.

Dove's giggle filled the room as she pulled May to her feet. "I want the bassinets to be on this side of the bed. That way it's easier to get up for the pup if we need to." May watched a pregnant Dove bounce around the room, listing where she wanted to put some of their stuff still in crates, and what they might have needed to move around.

May had never been happier.

Chapter 14

Dove was ecstatic for her evening meal with May later that night. They had been living together now for about two weeks, but lining up their schedule was difficult. Dove had fallen asleep quite a few times without May. She didn't enjoy that feeling, and tonight she wished to make it a bit of a point during their mealtime.

She hummed softly to the sounds of soft rain hitting their balcony. The doors were open, the hearth popping with fire and Dove was chopping fresh scallions. She had joined Eveleen for a walk in the garden earlier, who had shared how strong her and Taylor's mating bond had been recently, but that she could feel Taylor's fright most days. Dove could see the same in May. Neither of the Omegas were usually included in politics as they were to 'be protected' by the Alphas' orders but it was obvious there was something brewing.

"I think Taylor is only calm when I'm by her side. She spends all her time using our bond to protect me, but she forgets I can and have felt her for two years." Eveleen had rubbed her mark on the right side of her neck, looking over to Dove's unclaimed neck. She felt self-conscious, bringing her own hand up to rub her unblemished neck. She didn't know how she would feel about May's mark on her yet. She imagined it would happen, but was starting to realize anything she wanted, May would provide, and only if Dove wanted it. She put all of Dove's needs before her own needs and desires.

"When May comes home before bed, sometimes she seems more tense than I've seen her. I thought maybe it was us living together or me being pregnant, but when I start talking or we do things, that's only when she seems to relax." Dove had noticed May's tense postures when she entered their home, but once May settled in, she was comfortable. She had laughed at Dove's poorly told stories and smiled when Dove spoke about her day and she was joyous when they were talking about their future.

"Do things, or *do* things?" Eveleen gave a funny dance with her eyebrows as Dove rolled her eyes hard at her friend. She pushed her gently, which prompted a snarl from the guards behind her. She spun frantically to see one of the older Betas nearing her with ferocity. She almost cowered before the other guard stopped him. He whispered in the ear of the Beta and she couldn't hear what, but imagined it was something about her being the mother of May's child. She clutched her belly protectively. The Beta bowed deeply and apologized, but Dove would remember his face. She may be pregnant, but she wasn't soft.

"We have not been intimate since that first night, Eveleen. We've only really been together for over a month, and we've only lived together for two weeks. When I've tried to advance things, she shuts it down. I think she's still scared that she doesn't deserve me." Dove pinched the small skin close to her hips.

"There will be time, Dove." Eveleen had placed a hand on her shoulder. "When I moved here, Taylor barely touched me until the first few months. She would look at me and talk to me, but she wouldn't touch me. Not until that first time." Dove knew exactly what she was talking about. When Eveleen had been disrespected by a guard member, Taylor had not only banished him, but made it known to every single member of her kingdom that Eveleen was hers. As much as Eveleen disliked public gestures, it was what they had needed. Since then, Taylor barely left her side, but Dove knew it was out of love and not protection. The Omega had learned to protect herself.

"I want May to process everything in her own time. She's loved me for years and I'm not going to immediately dive into her trust and love and take it for my own when I haven't deserved it."

"You don't need to take her love, Dove, she's already giving it to you." She couldn't ignore what Eveleen said.

Dove hummed louder as she grabbed the scallions and threw them in the pot with the other vegetables— carrots, potatoes, and beans. She knew May would love the stew as much as she did. Dove cleaned up her work area because while May wouldn't mind, she did, and it would prompt May into a cleaning frenzy for her if she didn't clean up. The pitter patter of the rain continued as she looked around their home. Most of their clothes were ready to be washed as Dove scooped up the dirty fabrics to be taken to the wash.

"Dovely?" May entered the quarters, peeking her head in hesitantly, as if it wasn't her home too. Dove was facing the wardrobe but continued humming to herself as the strong Alpha approached behind her. "Hello, my sweet Dove."

May's arms encircled her waist hesitantly but secured Dove against her. Dove didn't know why May was acting so uncertain, but thought maybe Eveleen had spoken to Taylor, who spoke to May. Either way, Dove wanted tonight to be theirs. She melted into May's secure arms. With the height difference, the back of her head always hit just above May's collarbones.

"Hi." She spoke softly before turning in May's arms. "How was your day?" She circled her own arms around her muscular Alpha's waist. May leaned down and kissed her head. She snuggled closer into the warm body which smelled a bit like fire. With each inhale on May's uniform, she relaxed a little more. She was at peace.

"It will not compare to our evening. Let us enjoy the night?" May gripped her just a bit tighter before moving towards the balcony. She had her hands on the doors, ready to close them when Dove stopped her.

"Wait!"

"What? Is something wrong?" Both of May's hands were on the wooden handles. With the gray armor painting her, she was glowing. The tan skin and golden white hair were a glowing combination on her. Dove could sense how eager she was to get out of her uniform. She didn't typically wear it each day but today she had insisted on it.

"Nothing is wrong, honey. I just like to hear the rain." Dove held her hands behind her back as she watched May's realization form. She dropped both her hands before approaching.

"What else do you like?" She wasn't being condescending or sexual but was innocently asking about the small things Dove enjoyed. May loved Dove. She had been around her for years and observed all of her, but those small things Dove enjoyed couldn't be known unless told. At least not past the time May went to war. She understood what May was thinking. She moved towards one of the chairs in front of the hearth but didn't sit on it.

"You mean besides the sound of rain?" May nodded enthusiastically. She had never seen May this excited. "I really enjoy classical music. Every year or so when Taylor has a major event, she would agree to get the string quartet together for me to listen to. She said if I ever wanted to listen to them that I could, but I didn't want to abuse my relationship to the throne." May smiled as she sat in the chair in front of Dove listening to her. Her eyes had never shined so brightly.

"I also love the way that the grass feels under my feet when I walk around the garden or outside the livestock pen to tend to the animals." As Dove went on, listing the things she loved, she realized May was the top of it all.

"One of my favorite things though, is kneading bread. The way the dough folds so easily under my fingers and becomes this crunchy tasteful roll I created is such a complicated thing." Dove approached May and sat on her lap. "Was that what you wanted?"

May gathered her up in her arms, kissing her forehead. "It was. You smell so good."

Dove had started to notice small things about May. How she was in love with her scent, the pleasure she got from watching Dove whenever she got excited at her book. The way she folded their clothes at the end of the night with so much care.

"That's funny considering Taylor said I smell like you." She buried herself into May's side. Her legs dangled off the edge of the chair, while she sat perpendicular to her Alpha. May's nose was pressed right above her ear into her hair. She had taken a bath earlier and used her new hair scrub that smelled quite earthy. May just sat there, breathing her in like it was the only peace she had gotten all day.

"Will you tell me about your day?"

May's arms stiffened and she shook her head slightly. She so clearly didn't want to discuss her day, yet Dove wanted May to be comfortable coming home and resting. She tried so hard not to push but it was also who she was at her core. She was someone who pushed and didn't stop even when she should've stopped.

"What else do you like, Dovely?" May's head was tucked into Dove's neck.

"I like when you try to cook our morning meal. I like watching you sticking your tongue out of your mouth when you're thinking. The way you pretend you're not watching me while I'm reading at night. I like when you get home after I'm asleep and still curl up against me."

May nodded against her. Dove thought she was crying until May pulled her head back.

"I like watching you read." She pushed a strand of loose hair behind Dove's ear. It was clear to Dove that May was overwhelmed, but she didn't know by what. She tried her best to release comforting pheromones in the air as the pitter patter of the rain slowed down.

"Is that all?" Dove leaned forward, kissing May. It was soft but it drove Dove insane. She loved May's lips. They were always so soft, and so warm. Dove would lose herself in every kiss, but she didn't want that kind of intimacy right now. She just wanted to talk to her partner. Well, they hadn't labeled it yet, but Dove hoped May felt the same way.

"No, I like when you cook too. You are so effortless when you prepare food. You put your entire being into it. I cannot focus when I see you sway while you chop vegetables." May's words were barely above a whisper as she stared deeply into Dove's eyes. Dove felt as if May could see into her soul. She wanted to feel the same way and wanted May to know.

"Anything else?" Dove locked one arm around May's neck, tickling the hairs at the base of her neck. She was trying to find the courage to say how she felt.

"Sometimes before bed, you run your fingers up and down my arm without realizing. It makes me feel warm inside." May was mimicking her words by running her fingers along Dove's uncovered arm. It sent sparks into her nerves, making her feel alive.

Dove pressed her forehead to May's. It was a simple act, but she had never felt more at peace than in this moment.

"I love you May." She kissed May's nose before placing another gentle kiss on her lips. "You are my everything." She couldn't look in May's eyes. She knew they had said it once before, but she felt so much right now, it almost hurt.

"You, Dovely, are my whole heart. I love you too." They held each other for a few minutes, feeling peaceful and content. Dove still felt May's worry about whatever happened today, but she didn't want to press. She trusted May to tell her everything.

Chapter 15

At twenty-two weeks, May would attend one of Dove's doctor's appointments for the first time. She was supposed to be at the last appointment, but a political matter stopped her from being there. Dove had been disappointed, resulting in a quiet night until dawn. Dove could hardly stay mad at May when she attempted to make them their morning meal. She was getting better with each day, though.

Her taste had changed, which was normal this far into her pregnancy, at least according to her doctor. Dove had been an avid meat eater for all of her life, and working in the kitchen built her love for cooking, but she could barely stand looking at the food in front of her, let alone eating the meals provided for her. May had been excellent in taking the role of making most of their meals, but Kelsee helped her around the kitchen.

As of now she was gaining weight, which made her happy to think of the pup in her belly. She would momentarily get distracted and rub her tummy most of her days, but it made maneuvering more difficult. Kelsee had discussed the possibility of her working with the bakery items or a position where Dove would feel more secure in the upcoming weeks.

Dove still hadn't wanted to believe she was only carrying one pup, but with her weight gain, she had noticed that she was below target, and for that reason she was going to the doctor later that day. May would meet her there, but Dove assumed she would be disappointed if they only had one pup their first time around. Most Alphas were. They liked to believe their seeds held a great weight, so having only a single pup during a heat or rut meant they weren't as superior.

Slowly, Dove realized that she'd been thinking about what it would be like to be pregnant again. Sitting by the fireplace, she rubbed her swollen belly as she daydreamed about a litter of pups they might one day have. Would May even want more pups? Dove never thought she would want more than one, but thinking of little pups that were part of her and May made a warmth bloom in her chest.

Dove tried to shut down the thought that maybe May would only ever want one pup. She believed she would be okay with that, but with the conflicting thoughts running through her head, she had to close her book and move towards the balcony. The servants in the garden were moving around with efficiency as she gazed out at the mountain. Fog sat around the tips with each passing moment. Dove's hand found itself on the lower half of her body. She loved the pup in her body with her whole heart.

With the timing of the sun, she could see that her appointment was coming up, so she threw on a comfortable chemise to walk the corridors to the medical wing. Assuming May would just meet her there, she started her leisurely walk.

The whole way there she thought of May. Living together had been the easiest transition of her life. The Alpha always made sure they also had what they needed. Fresh clothes, ingredients to make morning and evening meals, a hot bath waiting for her. May was the most attentive person she had ever met, and Dove was in love with her. She was an absolute idiot for thinking that May was an arrogant and proud Alpha, when Dove knew who May was now. Even before their budding relationship, she had always been in proximity with May because of Taylor.

She should have seen how caring she was for Taylor and even knew how protective she was of Dove's safety. May had followed Dove during the night of her heat to protect her from the other Alphas swarming her. Dove had always been stubborn in her views when she set her mind to it. It was something she needed to work on, especially now that she was going to be a mother.

Eventually, she realized that she was at the front door of her doctor's office, when May met her there with her casual uniform on. The deep gray popped against May's fair skin. Her hair had been tied up in a braid, courtesy of Dove, but a few strands flew out.

"Hello." May leaned forward to place a short kiss on Dove's forehead before standing back with her hands tucked behind her back.

"That's how you greet the mother of your pup? Kind of lame, May." Dove was just playing, but after their lack of physical intimacy last night, she was desperate to feel

May on her. The Omega needed to have the Alpha. Taylor had recently told her that she smelled more and more like the Alpha in front of her, but she wasn't able to tell. Dove was just glad that everyone could tell who her Alpha was, because she was proud to be with her.

"I did not know if you were still upset with me." May whispered the words like she was embarrassed for her behavior last night, when she had done nothing wrong. Dove feared May wouldn't make it again, which resulted in the silence, and a lack of touch during their sleep.

Dove slept most peacefully when she was near May, but last night she had turned her back to the Alpha. Dove had adopted the side closest to the wardrobe and May towards the window balcony. While Dove was hesitant at first, May explained that if they ever needed to escape Dove would be closest to the door and able to grab the pups. They had slept perfectly well together, except when physical distance was required and her Omega craved the Alpha.

"I'm not upset with you, May." May couldn't even look at her, further confirming the thoughts Dove had, that May never thought she was enough. Dove needed to figure out how to show her Alpha that she was the perfect mate—or would be one day.

"You did not want me to hold you last night, and you would not kiss me this morning, which means you are upset with me." Dove couldn't see May's hands, but she knew that she was twisting her fingers. Her anxiety radiated off her scent, which urged Dove to reassure her.

"May, listen to me." Dove grabbed her arms, prompting May to give her her hands. "I am not upset with you, I promise. Last night I was worried something would come up again and you would miss this appointment."

"Which resulted in you being mad at me."

"May, I want to see how many pups we are having, and I didn't want you to miss the appointment. I think I just needed to distance myself last night in case that happened, but I swear, May. I am not mad. We promised communication and I should've made that a point last night." Dove stood on her tiptoes to rub her nose against May's scent gland, who let out a quiet, relieved sigh. "I love you, May, and I'm sorry for putting you in distress. You did nothing wrong."

May's arms circled Dove's waist, finally pulling her closer so that their bodies touched. Dove wrapped her hands around the Alpha's neck, twirling the little hairs as per usual. May's body relaxed against the Omega.

"I wish you would have told me. That way we could have done this last night." May pulled Dove up and kissed below her ear before nipping the skin. She kissed the corner of Dove's lips then placing a kiss on her lips. Before they could continue kissing more passionately, the doctor came out of his office, breaking apart their hallway affair.

"So sorry to interrupt, but I am on a tight schedule. If you two are ready, I can take you in here." May set Dove back down carefully, guiding her in the room. There was a chair for her to sit in. Vials of medication and multiple medical supplies she didn't recognize surrounded the room.

He usually just took her blood, checked her heart rate, made sure she was eating properly and the pup sounded okay. Today, though, they would find out the official number of pups Dove was carrying, even though Dove knew it was just the one.

"Update me, how have you been feeling?" He pulled out some parchment to record her symptoms. With her weight gain and change in appetite, she also had back aches from carrying the pup and a few cramps here and there. Explaining everything, he said she was on track with the weekly symptoms. May stood beside her, holding her hand a little too tightly each time the doctor spoke. She was such a worrier.

When the doctor pulled out the needle and vial to collect blood, May's loud growl filled the room, stopping the Beta doctor across from Dove.

"May, do you want to step out for this part?" Dove gripped her Alpha's hand, whose pheromones created a threatening atmosphere when a sharp object neared Dove. Even if she wasn't pregnant, she knew May would react this way.

"Why do you need to draw blood?" May glared at the needle. She was ready to attack anyone who would harm her pregnant Omega.

"The blood draw helps to see where the pups' health is at and to make sure Dove is also in good health. It can tell us what I can't see. Do I have your permission to continue, captain?"

Dove almost snarled at her doctor for asking permission from May to continue on Dove's body before she realized what it signified. He was asking because the protective Alpha was not only radiating threats, but May's scent covered all of Dove. It was there to warn others to leave her alone, because she belonged to May. Even though she hadn't been marked, the pup helped radiate May's smell. She grinned at the thought of everyone thinking of her as May's Omega. Even though she had initially disliked the idea of being marked by an Alpha, she now desperately wanted May's bite.

"Yes, but I cannot look." Gently touching her lips to Dove's forehead, she kept their heads connected at a perpendicular angle, looking away from the scene. The needle went into Dove's vein, causing her to wince as May whispered a few sweet words in her ear. Soon enough it was over, and he was bandaging up her arm.

"Was there anything else you were concerned about?" He positioned himself in front of the couple with a perceptive look.

"I was wondering if you would be able to tell us how many pups we were having?" May gave her another hand squeeze. May was tucked right by her side now, as they had gravitated towards each other throughout the appointment. The feel of May's thumb rubbing patterns over her hand while she sat and explained her pregnancy was natural, everything Dove had been craving over her last few visits.

Their doctor raised a thick eyebrow at them. "I thought you wanted to wait until the birth?" Dove and May made eye contact, prompting a subtle nod from May. She would not do anything May was uncomfortable with.

"I've been thinking, and I would rather be prepared knowing how many pups versus the day of." That was not unnecessarily true, but she had just been processing more recently.

"I understand. Going from no children to multiple is definitely a switch. Let me get the stethoscope so I can listen for the heartbeats and confirm." Dove knew that he also knew how many pups she was pregnant with and that they were putting the show on for May. She didn't mind. He exited the room, and Dove desperately wanted May to hold her.

"However many pups, we will be okay. We will be able to handle all the pups."

"Would you be disappointed if it was only one pup?" Dove craned her neck to look up into the green eyes. May's soft hairs had escaped her braid, and Dove reached out to play with them. As Dove's fingers tangled with the hair, she noticed that May's look was a cross between introspective and confused. May smoothed down the ginger hairs that were stuck to her head.

"Do you really think I could be disappointed in you or our child? I do not care if it is one or a million. I will admit the thought of spoiling a single pup during their first year has kept me up at night. I will dress her in the finest fabrics and the most delicious food when she gets older, and the thought of you with our pup has sent me into a frenzy. But it would be so much fun if we have multiple pups—playing with them after work but teaching each of them to fight and eventually having them gang up on me all at once would be joyous. Whether it is a single pup or multiples this time around, I will be ecstatic, because they are ours." May's words screamed truth, but Dove could barely hear them over the excitement pounding through her veins. They were going to be a family. They *were* a family.

"You think it's a girl?" A smile broke Dove's face.

Before they could kiss, the doctor came back, holding his stethoscope. "This will be slightly cold on the skin, but once I have determined the number of heartbeats, I'll let you know." He sat down in a chair close to Dove's belly before pressing the cold metal to her flush skin.

Dove looked into May's eyes. She was so alive right now. Here she sat with her favorite person, who helped create a life with her. With May standing above her, she let loose all the emotions her Omega was feeling. Eventually, he pulled the metal away. He looked into both of their eyes, folding the stethoscope around his neck.

"It seems that you are only pregnant with one pup." Dove couldn't stop the happy images May described from flooding her brain when May leaned down and kissed her.

Chapter 16

The twenty-eighth week of Dove's pregnancy had to be the worst. After fourteen weeks of living with Dove, May had never been so overwhelmed. Many of the smaller villages were in civil disruption, and May had to send a few dozen of her trainees into them. There were a few riots but only one official death amongst the people who were against the throne. Kaden and Zoe were past the training stages and official guards in the army, leaving May with no training responsibilities.

On the way into her office, she saw all of her new recruits standing at the center of the mat. She had yet to find any two who stood out to her. May only had three things on her mind these days—Dove, their unborn pup, and an impending war threatening to break out in their country.

May worked at her desk for the majority of the day until the quick knock on the door startled her, causing her to mess up her army placement sheet. She could smell the pheromones radiating off of Dove's body as she pushed through the door. She had started wearing May's cloaks to conceal her swollen belly. May had threatened to cut the bottom of one of them because Dove kept dragging it along and tripping because of it.

May stood instantly and practically raced to Dove's side.

"Is something wrong? Is the pup okay?" She placed her hand on the underside of Dove's belly, almost dropping to her knees to listen to the slow heartbeat.

They would lie on the bed together every night, and while Dove read, May would occasionally let her head rest on Dove's belly, all while making sure it was comfortable for Dove. It was the time she felt closest to her family, to the two most important girls in her life.

"The pup is fine, honey. I just wanted to bring you some lunch." Dove had started referring to May as 'honey' a few weeks ago, which gave her heart palpitations every time. Dove held a basket of bread, ready to be spread with jam, and some salami. Dove's days had been spent mostly attending to everything except cooking, which caused her some distress at first.

She was slowly starting to realize, after talking with May about it, that it was for the best.

"Here, come sit on my comfortable chair, baby." As Dove sat, May removed her shoes, ready to give her a foot rub but was stopped when Dove pushed the bread in her direction.

"You better not rub my feet before touching the bread I made you." Soft hands pulled May up to sit on the armrest of the chair. She leaned up, silently begging May for a kiss, who happily complied.

Starlight burst behind her eyes when their lips touched. Her neck craned as she slipped her tongue into Dove's mouth. The pheromones Dove produced started radiating into the room with each kiss, and the only thing stopping them was the Omega breaking apart with an uncomfortable groan. May almost jumped into action, ready to scoop Dove up and race her to the medical wing.

"It's just a small contraction, May." Another painful sound left Dove as she shifted in the chair.

"How long have you been having them?" May had been talking to one of her guards who recently had a pup, asking what the best way to help with contractions was and what warning signs were there. She learned that as they got closer to the birth date, the contractions would be closer together and more painful. The thing that helped him most was a bath or a massage.

"It has only been a few days, but they are extremely far apart, honey. There is nothing to worry about. I still have ten weeks to go."

"How about when I get home, I draw you a nice warm bath. I got some lavender recently and salts that will make you feel better." May scooped up a piece of bread from the basket. She needed to distract herself with something from the thought of her pup coming early. Their bassinet still wasn't ready, and they only had a few items for the pup.

Dove stretched her legs out and flexed her toes through her socks. Her soft chemise outlined her pregnant stomach with the pink stretch marks while her hair was tied up so it wouldn't block her face. Her freckled nose was shining under the burning gas lamp in May's office. May was unsure if it was her scent bleeding off Dove or the physical evidence of her on Dove's body, but every time she gazed upon her, she felt luckier than before. She kept thinking this was a dream, and that she'd wake up soon.

"I wish I could take that bath now. After how much I sweat in bed last night, I was ready to rinse off this morning but we both got out of our quarters so fast." When the sun rose earlier that morning, May was ushered to a royal meeting with multiple city officials and the Queen herself. She had no time to make her Omega breakfast or wash herself.

Their sex life had been fairly dormant with each passing week of Dove's pregnancy, but that didn't mean their intimacy was any less. In fact, it was more than usual. Dove was extremely touch-oriented, refusing to be more than a few feet apart from May whenever they were alone. It felt to May as though she was a part of Dove's body, and she loved it. During the evenings, they would sit by the fire or on the balcony reading together with May studying reports, but their skin was always touching. Dove would curl their legs together, or have May against her back, joined as one.

The only time their sex life was affected was about two weeks ago when she went into a rut. Dove almost begged May to knot her, but May's rut this time around was unpredictable and painful, so she slept in the quarters next to theirs. It had an adjoining door where their pup would sleep in a few years. It was a perfect test run, except for the fact that her Alpha was clawing her skin to push Dove down to the bed and fuck her as violently, and lovingly, as she could.

"If I did not have to fill out this paperwork now, I would take you home and draw it for you. As for now, let us eat your delicious meal." Dove nodded silently, bringing all her food out on May's desk. The Alpha had pushed the parchments aside so she could have Dove's food in front of her. Dove collected some of the documents, but May wished she hadn't. The Omega's face showed concern and sorrow as she skimmed the details.

"There are more requests to send troops out to the far north? There's nothing out there but the ruins, why would anyone want that? Have you discussed this with Taylor?" The inner fight of her Omega was starting to present itself. She did not want Dove's blood pressure to rise to an unhealthy rate, but she desperately needed to talk about this. May couldn't go to her best friend because the Queen would take over, but Dove would remain loyal to her.

"Apparently the land around the Ruins of Luiza has been deemed as an area that could be dangerous and welcomed for rebels of the throne to gather. It is not a permanent movement, but Taylor asked me to send just a few to make sure the location is secure. Zoe is going to attend the party, but even sparing this many soldiers during the current political state is concerning."

"May, are you scared?" Dove broke some of the bread and spread the jam on a piece before handing it to May. She took it willingly, enjoying the tart taste of the berries and the softness of the bread.

"The only thing I am concerned about is having a little pup." She tried to play it off as a joke, but there was some truth to it. Dove shifted uneasily across from May. All her senses were on overdrive with the pup, but even so she would be able to tell how nervous Dove was.

"May, please speak to me honestly. I can sense how stressed you've been, and I hadn't wanted to push it, but if it's getting this serious then I need you to tell me the truth." Dove's pleading tore down May's barriers.

"Taylor has started reallocating money with the treasury so she can figure out a way to lower taxes again. If I have to fill out one more form for swapping my army around, I *will* lose it."

Dove took slow bites of her food, bouncing her knee. "Will you have to go out there yourself?" Dove's hazel eyes avoided May's. Her Alpha immediately stepped up to comfort her scared Omega. She would not let her Omega feel upset in her presence if she could help it.

"I am not going to leave you. Whether it settles down or gets worse, I will be here with you and the pup. *You* are my duty. *You* are my life." May had moved to position herself between Dove's knees. She had stopped crossing her legs so May could easily maneuver herself between them on her knees. Her Omega's pheromones were so close to her nose as she kissed the pregnant belly. Dove reached down to thread her fingers softly into May's locks.

"Have you ever thought about stepping down?"

May felt a punch in her gut from those words. Did Dove really doubt her abilities? Recently she had been feeling increasingly overwhelmed with her position, yet she never would have accepted it if she didn't think she could do it. Taylor thought she could, but now the woman she loved thought she couldn't. It hurt and she recoiled. She didn't want Dove to see the hurt, so she hid it as well as she could, burying her head closer to the pregnant belly. Yet Dove could always read her, now more than ever.

Dove gently tugged her locks so their eyes would meet. She motioned for May to join her on the chair.

"May, that came out wrong. I do not doubt your abilities as Captain of the army. You have done an amazing job over the years, and you have earned your position. What I meant was that you've always disliked the political aspect and love training. Maybe you could talk to Taylor and work out something, so you are less involved in the matters you dislike." Dove's chair was big enough so that she was tucked into Dove's side and each word resonated in her soul.

Had she really done such a poor job hiding her dislike in politics? Dove's words had truth to them, but stepping down at such a critical moment in their country's safety would be the most cowardly thing she could do.

"These are unsteady times, Dovely. I absolutely cannot discuss this with Taylor when there is so much uneasiness in our country. The transition period is more important than my concerns. It is my job to handle the placement of our troops for the wellbeing of others." The words came out softer than she intended. Dove was still playing with her hair while her other hand ran up and down her wrist.

"You are the most noble person I've met, May. I understand what you're saying and I'm not trying to force you to make this decision, but I know you, May, and I know your heart lies with building connections with your army, not doing paperwork." She gestured to the mess on her desk. "I understand the job comes with both and I've felt how stressed you've been. I know you don't think this disruption in our villages is going anywhere, but I think your skills are best used on the people, not the politics. I also know Taylor would understand."

May snuggled her head closer to her Omega's scent gland. She smelled so good, it was comforting. "Can we discuss something else, please?" May tightened her arm around Dove.

"How about we talk about more names?" May rolled her eyes, causing Dove to laugh. They had been extremely indecisive when it came to a name and since they didn't know if it was a boy or girl, they had a multitude. May was fairly certain that it would be a little girl, but they would have to wait and see.

"You got yourself a deal."

***

After discussing and a few gentle arguments on pup names, May was summoned to Taylor's office where they went over more strategy. At this point in the day, May was ready for her evening with Dove.

The talk that May and Taylor were having about the army quickly devolved into a screaming match between the Alphas.

"I understand that you are allocating as best as you can, May. However, this isn't cutting it." Taylor slammed her newest plan on the desk, causing the Alpha in May to growl. It was low and rumbly, but it was a warning to Taylor. Taylor was aggravated with May, yet May was equally upset. In all her years of being friends with Taylor, she had never felt this aggression towards her.

"I have been doing my best, Taylor, but the situation keeps changing daily, and you are not updating me fast enough!"

Taylor placed both palms on her desk and leaned forward, practically snarling. "Then maybe you should do your job and go out in the field."

May was taken aback at the statement but refused to wince.

"Absolutely not. My job is to oversee the training of recruits and to make sure all the papers line up with what is needed. I am not about to go into an uncertain situation when my Omega is pregnant and about to give birth. I thought you would not want that either, considering Dove is your best friend." May was the older Alpha, but Taylor held more authority. Taylor titled her chin upwards, a gulp lining her throat, but she didn't back down.

"I expect you to do your job as the captain of my army, not be at the beck and call of a single pregnant Omega." That was the last straw for May. The last few months had been driving May insane. She didn't care about the protection of her kingdom; she only cared about her family! If Taylor couldn't settle royal matters without her army, maybe she shouldn't be Queen.

"What the hell is your problem, Taylor? Dove is ten weeks away from giving birth, and you want to send me to the ruins, which is a multi-day journey where I could be put in danger, or maybe killed? You cannot be that arrogant." She threw her hands in the air, resisting the urge to let her Alpha take control.

They stood there, staring at each other. Maybe Dove had been correct in May stepping down. She was only thirty and her job was killing her. She had never felt like enough, and this job made her feel even less. How was she supposed to provide for anyone at all if she couldn't even protect her country with a few pieces of paper?

"What did you say?" Taylor moved around her desk to stand in front of May, who had a few inches on her Queen. She wasn't playing games, letting out a threatening sound. May was too tired to deal with this. Avoiding Taylor's gaze, she stared at the greenery outside the Queen's window.

"I apologize, Your Highness. I can send Caleb and a few of my trusted trainees to assess up close and come back with a proper report." Tucking her hands behind her back, May straightened. Both their jaws were tightened as they stood tensely on edge.

"And if I ordered you to go to the ruins yourself?" A royal eyebrow raised at her best friend. Was she seriously asking her to choose between her duty as her Captain and her loyalty to Dove? There was nothing in this world that could draw her away from Dove's side while she was pregnant.

"Then I guess you will have to decide whether or not you are going to charge me with treason as the love of my life grows our child." The staring contest between the two lasted for an uncomfortable amount of time. The two Alphas were trying to dominate the other and the room reeked of unpleasant pheromones. She could see that Taylor was considering it and that her Alpha had taken over every part of Taylor's mind.

"You're dismissed, *Captain*." The words had never held so much venom as Taylor spewed it at her. May had to resist launching a verbal attack at her closest friend. She had no idea what her problem was, but her line of questioning was uncalled for.

She left the office, deciding it was time to retire to her home for the day. She could not believe that Taylor would force her to choose between her country and her Dove. It may be wrong as she was sworn in as an official of Taylor's royal court, but Dove was the one person in her life she would die for, and soon her pup would be the other.

She was furious by the time she reached her quarters, practically slamming the wooden door shut as she entered the living space. Before May could catch her breath, an overwhelming smell of concern filled her senses. Her eyes snapped over to Dove who lay on the bed.

"Whatever is wrong, my Dove?" May crossed the rest of the room in two steps. Hurrying towards her Omega, she had to resist throwing her over her shoulder and going to the medical wing, *again.* Instead, she sat near Dove's legs, brushing her thumb along Dove's ankle and feeling some of Dove's anxiety disappear.

Dove was laying on her back, her hands splayed on her stomach with wide eyes. The sound of her name must have jolted Dove back to her senses.

"I think something is wrong with the pup." The hand that lay guarding her belly started moving back and forth. "I could not feel her moving after our lunch. She has been very active every day and I'm..." She trailed off, meeting May's eyes. "I'm scared, May."

May shifted on the edge of the bed before she placed both her knees on it. The air was alive with its own emotion. May knew she had to keep her own growls and scent in check while she comforted her Omega, but her Alpha needed to make sure her pup was okay. She tried to keep the warring parts of herself together when she realized they both wanted the same thing. Her Alpha always needed to provide for her Omega, to protect her, give her everything she needed, and dominate her, sometimes. May wanted those things too, but she needed to reassure Dove. The part of Dove that was pregnant, was fearful for her pup and seemed to have been driven from a place of worry.

Up until now, her entire pregnancy had been smooth according to the doctor. They had no reason to worry. May kept that thought at the forefront of her mind, along with Dove's worries. Whether irrational or not, they were real, and May would address Dove's every thought. She completely forgot about Taylor now that she was with her family.

Crawling up over Dove's swollen belly, she pressed a chaste kiss on her Omega's lips. She continued to press a few more down her jaw, and Dove let out a soft sigh. Her hands shot up to May's hair, her body immediately softening when May nuzzled the scent gland on Dove's neck. May inhaled her scent. It was still just as sweet as usual—like honey. She peppered a few kisses on it. May pressed her forehead against Dove's, before finally pulling away, but her calming pheromones curled around Dove.

She continued her journey down Dove's body, stopping at her peak to press a few kisses in the same spot she always had, right above Dove's belly button where the lifeline to her pup lay. Their pup would be joining the world soon, the harsh world that May would protect him or her from. She thought of Taylor's worry about the potential uprising. Pushing all worries out of her mind, she focused on the moment.

While she was convinced the pup was a girl, May didn't care either way. Soon, a pup that she and Dove had created together would see the world. She would protect her pup and Dove with her life. May pressed one ear against Dove's belly, making herself as comfortable as she could.

"What are you doing?" Dove asked, her voice airy.

"Shh, I am listening to our pup." The thrumming of Dove's body hit her ears. She had done this many times since they had moved in together. Dove would run her fingers through May's hair with an anxious purr, and a low grumble would build in May's chest. She could occasionally hear their pup moving around and even feel the kicking. A small smile bloomed on her face.

"Well?"

"That pup's heartbeat is slow, but she is thriving in there." She looked up at her pregnant Dove, and all her worries went away.

It was right then that May realized she should step down. When Taylor confronted her earlier, she felt nothing but anger towards her best friend. She only felt joy now, and it was not from her job. She enjoyed training Kaden and Zoe, but all her confidence was paired with the paperwork and it caused her to doubt everything she did. Right now, in their home with her little family, May was whole.

"How about I go ahead and draw you that bath?"

"Only if you join me?" Dove pushed up on her elbows. A wicked look painted Dove's freckled face. She could barely stop the arousal in her pheromones when May smelled slick drifting from Dove.

"What about your pain?" Her brows knit together in concern.

"You know that sex is a great distraction, right?" May eyed the desire glistening down Dove's thighs. Her cock sprang to life in her trousers, pulsing rapidly when Dove's hand wandered towards her wet pussy. May's own scent radiated from Dove's body. Her possessive nature took over. This was her Omega teasing her.

"I will distract you, my Omega. You just have to tell me how." She walked off towards their washroom to start the bath. The luxury of living in a joint quarter closer to the Queen came with the benefit of having hot water fill their tub.

May gathered up the lavender and salts she had purchased a few days ago. She graciously poured it in the tub so it would dissolve in the water faster.

Grabbing the fluffiest drying cloth they had, she set it aside for Dove after their wash. She was about to turn and grab her Omega when Dove walked in behind her.

She was completely naked. Stretch marks glowed around her belly and thighs. *Glorious.* May wanted to kiss her every inch of them, and she would. Her freckled skin was a bit pink in some places and tan in others. Her fiery hair was down in loose waves. May wanted to grip it with Dove on her knees. But what turned May on most was the slick literally dripping down her thighs. She could smell Dove's sweet scent from the opposite side of the room.

Dove strode across the room, knowing just what she was doing to May. She swayed her hips, running her hands over her pregnant tummy. May chewed her bottom lip as her cockhead pulsed along with her heart. Dove stopped right in front of her, gripping her hard cock through her trousers. May's jaw trembled as she held eye contact with Dove. She resisted rocking her pelvis up into Dove's hand as that secondary pulse continued to grow in her cock.

"I want these off, my Alpha. I want to feel your cock on my skin." She rubbed slowly as May pulled her beige tunic off. Dove flicked her thumb back and forth over the bulge. May felt her pre-come dribble out of her cock while Dove placed her thighs on May's leg. Here she was with her pregnant Omega whose pheromones were mixed with hers. And inside of her belly was May's pup. She growled, every inch of her cock straining.

"I will give you my cock once you are in the water, Dovely." As much as she wanted Dove in the bath, she couldn't stop herself from gripping her Omega's waist to help give Dove more friction on her leg. Her cockhead was starting to throb uncomfortably when their lips met in a passionate kiss. Every inch of her skin was on fire with each pulse and moan from Dove. May opened her eyes to look down at her Omega, who was using her leg to get herself off. Her beautiful bump between them set May off.

"Oh fu-fuck Dove, I am going to—" She felt her orgasm ripple through her body, tightening her hands on Dove, who leaned forward to capture her lips once more. Her lower body trembled and shook as Dove continued grinding against her. Desperate moans from Dove echoed around the chamber as May's come coated her lower body, which was still fully covered. She was never able to resist Dove but spraying her come in her pants was a new low.

May had to turn her head to the side to avoid the embarrassment she was feeling. Her cheeks burned with a pink tint as Dove slowed her hips. She couldn't help the possessive nature that flowed through her when she saw Dove, or the fire in her blood. Yet she just came without providing her very pregnant Omega with anything. She was ashamed. Her Alpha started to withdraw when Dove spoke.

"That was so hot, baby." Dove tangled her hands in the little blonde hairs at the edge of her neck. "I think I'm ready to join you in the bath now." She toyed with the edge of May's trousers and pulled them down. Her lower body was covered with the cream from her seed. "If I could, I would get on my knees and lick you up. But I think I'd rather just have you do it again, but in me."

May carefully took her hand to make sure Dove didn't slip. The Omega lowered into the tub, her naked body glowing. The stretch marks all over her body shined when she hit the water. When Dove was fully submerged, she drifted towards the edge of the tub, biting her lips and motioning for May to join her.

Slowly, she entered the water herself, floating over towards Dove to start kissing her. The warmth of the water enveloped her. They slipped into their usual routine of Dove sitting on May's lap and their tongues in a passionate dance. Over the past few weeks, this was the most they had done. They made out for a while before Dove spoke.

"I want you to take me from behind while I sit on your lap. I want you to pound your cock into me, Alpha." When Dove slipped into calling May 'Alpha,' she was astonished but gave into her base nature.

"Anything for my Omega." She shifted in the tub with her back against the porcelain. Dove sat on her lap, not quite ready for her. May wrapped her safely in her arms and gently pressed kisses to her gland. She applied pressure, sucking the supple skin between her lips.

"Does that feel good?" The Omega shivered under her hold. May took that as a sign to grip her even tighter. Her murmurs vibrated against Dove's skin.

"It's perfect, Alpha. I'm ready." Although they were in the water, she knew Dove's slick would still be enough for them.

With Dove in her arms, the warm water engulfed both of them, heating their skin. May skipped the foreplay, which usually consisted of coating her cock with the slick at Dove's pussy, and carefully slid her cock into the tight opening. Dove melted back into May's arm as her Omega's inner walls slowly gripped the length of her cock. The tight pussy was pulling her in further.

"Your pussy is so tight, Dove." May pushed the wet hair off her temple. Placing a gentle kiss below her ears, May moved her nose to the mating gland. She adored taking Dove from behind while they were connected in the bath, but she wanted to see the look of pleasure on Dove's face.

"Please stretch me, Alpha! I need your knot, to keep me open!" Dove's hand slipped behind her head to grab a handful of the golden locks. She turned to see May, almost begging. "Please kiss me May. I need to feel every inch of you."

May pressed her lips to Dove's before slowly pulling out and thrusting in. She gripped Dove's small waist to pin their hips together. Dove broke their lips in a silent whimper as May slowly pushed in. She savored every inch of her warmth before she started her thrusts.

Pushing her hips up into Dove's, she felt herself pressing into where she had not yet reached, while Dove's moans broke the silence in the room. May's knot slowly grew as the bath water sloshed, overflowing the sides of the tub with each almost violent thrust into her Omega's slick pussy.

With every movement up into the velvety walls, May gave her Omega everything. May held Dove against her, her hands pressing them together as one. May's thick cock slid a bit unevenly while Dove tried to grip her thighs.

"Oh May!" Dove cried out, arching her back, before May lured her closer. If the sound of their bodies slapping was audible, it would have been music. May's Alpha furiously worked herself in and out of Dove, whose walls clenched around her, her knot now fully swollen. She didn't want to hurt her Omega, but she needed release.

"Are you ready to take my knot, Dovely?" she growled low as the water continued splashing against their bodies.

"Yes, please May! Please, Alpha. Pound into me. Release your seed."

"You feel so good. Gonna give you another." She grit the words out as her come burst into Dove. Her Omega's walls clenched, leaving May unable to move as Dove started trembling above her.

"May! May, I love you." She would have said it back if she didn't come again while Dove shook, grabbing her curls. Her knot tied them together, but Dove was still producing slick.

"Does my baby feel better?" May moved her hands, gripping Dove's waist to hold her bloated belly. She rubbed slowly, placing as many kisses as she could on Dove's neck. "Did I help calm you?"

Chapter 17

May was a giver, and Dove was about to give back. Once they were settled on the bed and dried, Dove crawled on top of her Alpha, bracketing her hips with both thighs. Leaning over May, her naked belly rubbed against May's hardening cock. The pre-come was already glistening on her tip and arousal poured from Dove's core. She wasn't focused on that though as she captured May's soft lips. Parts of her body were covered in scars, her hands calloused from fighting, but May's lips were soft every time, as if they had never been kissed. Dove slipped her tongue in May's mouth, gathering a moan from them both.

May's hands reached out to Dove's breasts, palming each one but with less pressure than before. They had grown in size recently but May holding them now made it all worth it. She continued battling May's tongue for dominance but gave up when May pinched her nipple teasingly. She had to release May's lips to let out a moan. May leaned up to take a breast in her mouth when Dove remembered what she wanted.

Gently capturing both of May's hands, she guided them above the Alpha's head. Her long hair hadn't had time to dry so it was tightly curled.

"What—what are you doing?" May breathed out her words with little air, like she couldn't believe this was happening. May flexed her hands to interlock their fingers together, holding them above her head, waiting for Dove to explain. She could see the inner Alpha holding down a snarl from being dominated this way. With the lack of sex life, Dove could only imagine how hard it was to control her primal nature.

"I want you to tell me, my Alpha. What was your biggest fantasy of us being together?" Dove nipped right below May's ear, trying to ignore the overwhelming arousal from her pheromones. Through numerous conversations since they had gotten together, she knew how much May fantasized about her. "Tell me."

May's whimper was all that was left of her tame nature. Her Alpha's cock throbbed and leaked pre-come as May leaned up to watch Dove. They hadn't explored

May's cunt yet, but Dove was craving it more and more, just not tonight. May let her hands be held down, but when she let her breath coat Dove's ear, Dove realized even though she was on top, the Alpha was in charge now.

"I imagined you bouncing on my cock while I lie here on my back, letting you do all the work and when you finally crumbled above me, dropping your trembling body over mine, I would sink my teeth into your mating gland, tying us together for eternity."

While some of May's confession brought uncertainty to Dove, the majority was arousal. Her excitement pooled out of her, coating May's body. While their physical intimacy was lacking over the past few weeks, Dove knew she was going to be with May forever. The change in the relationship was easy for her. Spending nights with May, waking up in her arms, and eating their morning meals together had quickly become their routine, even when they hadn't shared quarters. Now that they did, Dove could picture it clearly—what their life held in store for them, but they had yet to talk about mating.

"It seems like my Alpha has a very vivid imagination." With one more kiss, Dove raised herself up as May watched her like she was a precious piece of art. The tenderness in her eyes was what drove Dove to continue her movements. The pheromones in the room were that of connection, one built out of trust, joy, and love.

Positioning May's dripping cock below her entrance, she took one second to herself before practically impaling herself on the hard length. May's hands swiftly gripped her waist as Dove adjusted to the thickness of May. She threw her head back as May's low guttural moan caused the Omega great pride. Every time she drew pleasure out of her Alpha, her Omega felt fulfilled. She locked her gaze with the Alpha's green eyes and began to fulfill May's fantasy.

The excitement from both of them made the next part easier as she bounced on her Alpha's cock. She brought her hips up and down, ass bouncing while her inner walls gripped the length. Just as May fantasized, she let Dove do all the work, but it looked almost painful for her, so Dove decided to give her something to do.

"I want you to play with your nipples, please." May's eyes glinted at her as she slowly reached up, touching her dusky brown nipples. Her body glowed under the low light in the room, highlighting the swell of May's breasts. Dove wanted to take one in her mouth and bite them, but that wasn't in the fantasy. The plan was to continue pleasuring herself with May's body.

"Anything for you, Omega. But if you stop riding my cock, I will stop playing."

Dove gave a quick nod, rolling her hips before using May's body to slide up and down. They each increased their paces, creating the obscene sound of bodies slapping together. Overwhelmed with the pheromones coming from her Alpha, and the feel of May's cock buried in her, she started quaking. Her thighs tightened when May encouraged her on.

"Come on my cock, Dovely. Coat me with everything you have got, baby, and I will come for you."

The promise of her Alpha's come in her was enough to break Dove apart. She felt herself tightening around May before she sank down as deeply as she could on May's cock. The knot at the base of May's cock remained outside of Dove, but the final few inches left a good burn while she shivered around May. Just as promised, May pushed up into her, releasing a cry as her come spurt into Dove, causing a second wave of orgasm to crash over her.

Dove felt fulfilled as the Alpha's hard length released multiple streams of come into her. Every spurt filled her already pregnant tummy. Still connected, Dove leaned forward, letting her shaking body rest on her Alpha. A content purr built in her throat as she thought about the next part of May's fantasy. After a few moments and the aftershocks of their orgasm calmed, Dove breathed her next thoughts to life.

"I want you to claim me, May. Bite me. Let everyone know who I belong to until the end of my days." With their height differences, her mating gland rested just above May's collarbones. They would have to shift positions around to achieve the ritual but May froze under her.

"This is just in-the-moment talking, Dovely. You cannot possibly want that." A calloused hand ran down Dove's side as her heart broke a little.

When would May realize that Dove only wanted her? And only her forever? When would she understand that the caring Alpha below her was everything she ever desired? But May blew all her dreams out of the water. May was the one person on this planet who put her every need forward and Dove needed May to realize that. She just didn't know how.

"I am going to pull out." May's naked body moved below her, their sweaty skin sliding together as her Alpha released her. They would probably need another wash after this. The moment was still in the air, but Dove could feel how it had changed. May's scent remained joyful yet cautious.

Dove felt May's hands rub the bottom of her neck. Red hair stuck to her skin as they sat in silence. Dove pressed a chaste kiss on her Alpha's collarbone. She lay against May, trying to be as honest as possible with her pheromones.

"How can I prove to you that you are enough for me? I know these past few months you've been doubting yourself because that's what you're used to, and I would never stop you from seeing your pup but if I didn't want to be with you, I *wouldn't*, May. This pup brought us together, but I don't have to be with you romantically. Every morning that I get to wake up with you is like a dream. Every night that I get to feel you beside me as we fall asleep brings me peace. When I feel our pup kick, I think about us, that first time together and who we made and will raise. May, you are everything I want and need in my life. I want you as my co-parent, my Alpha, my wife...even my Mate."

May shifted below her, sitting up, causing Dove to do the same as well. Maybe presenting the idea was going to scare May, but Dove trusted her.

"Do you really want that?" May twisted the furs on their bed with her fingers, but she wouldn't meet Dove's eyes. Dove put her finger under May's chin to draw their eyes together.

"May...I want you from the moment we met till the rest of our days and everything after." May released a tiny cry before leaning forward to collapse on Dove.

"You are all I have ever wanted in my life, Dove. I would happily take you as my mate because my soul has been waiting since the day we met." May, for once, crawled on Dove's lap. Her cock was completely limp, and Dove was glad because as intimate as this moment was, it wasn't driven by sexual desire. However, she expected the need to feel May inside her again after the ritual.

"Maybe our pup was the fates making me realize we belong together." Dove cradled her fragile May in her arms. The big strong Alpha was reduced to sobs with every word Dove spoke. No one had ever loved her like May, and no one ever would.

"Honey, we can wait and do this later if you are too overwhelmed." She stroked her wet hair while gripping her lower back tightly. May broke their skin-to-skin contact, leaving Dove feeling absent. She was still on her lap, but without the skin contact after their passion made Dove feel lonely. She wanted to feel everything May had to offer, every thought, every feeling, every moment, forever.

"If you want I will, but otherwise I want to bury my teeth into your gland while you do the same."

"May, you do not have to take my mark." Dove knew how much May loved her, but the idea of an Alpha in high rankings wearing a claim mark was mostly unheard of. They mostly had them hidden, if the mated pair even shared marks.

"If you do not take my mark, Dovely, then you are not getting your own. You have been written in my soul since the first day we met, so I might as well let everyone else see it. If you want your teeth buried beneath my skin, you will mark me as your equal." Tangling her fingers in the golden halo, Dove framed May's face before she leaned in. Everything about May was perfect. She had the most gorgeous smile, the prettiest laugh, and she was the most noble person she knew. May brought her a joy she had never known, and she wanted to be around her for eternity.

"I love you, May Charlotte. There is no one on this planet who would ever make me feel the way you do. I am so excited to be your mate." Dove didn't look May in the eyes as she ran her tongue over the gland where May's Alpha pheromones bled from. She inhaled them, then breathed out. May had her hands around her lower back, so they were locked together. May was currently sniffing her hair, probably trying to soak up her natural scent, before she was overwhelmed with the mixed scent their pup created.

"You, Dovely Fortenberry, are the reason I live, and I will spend every day of my life being the person you deserve." May positioned her own teeth over Dove's gland. She could feel the gentle breath coating her neck. "I love you, Dovely. I will always love you." May didn't say anything else before she pierced the precious skin.

For once May didn't doubt herself as she bit one of the most fragile parts of Dove's body. Dove instantly thrummed to life, feeling her Alpha. Her cells were alive with activity with the body below her. Everything clicked into place while May moaned against her neck. She was dizzy with happiness but suddenly wanted May to feel the same way. She dipped forward, finding May's own mating gland and burying her teeth in it. Omegas' marks were typically hidden, but she refused to let anyone else think May was available for the taking. This perfect Alpha was *hers*.

May released a roar when Dove's teeth sank below her skin. She immediately thought she did something wrong until May gave her the most violent kiss of her life.

"Mine. Mine forever. My perfect Omega, created for me, existing for me." Every one of May's words were choked out, accompanied with a violent breath. Through

their joint bond they would feel every emotion, and they would be together every moment.

They were one.

The feeling of May's radiating beneath her bones was increased tenfold when they were equally claimed by each other. May's teeth in her mating gland was stronger than any orgasm. It felt like every *I love you* combined. Dove couldn't think of the last time she was more satisfied. She was in her home, with her mate in her arms, after a perfect night of sex, and she would soon give birth to their pup. She radiated in the feeling of falling asleep with her mate, never feeling so content in her life.

Chapter 18

The first time May had ever been put on the battlefield with a sword was when she was freshly fifteen. She had killed her first man that same day and it had changed her from that day forward. There was not a moment since then that was as scary or threatening as standing in front of the door that belonged to her mate's parents.

Dove's hand was safely tucked into hers, and it made her feel a bit better. The small thumb gently rubbed back and forth over her own hand. As of three days ago, they were officially mated, and nothing had ever felt more right in her life. Every single decision she had made in her thirty years led to taking Dove as her mate, mother of her child, and one day, wife.

"They already know you, May. They have always thought you were a caring person and now you are the sire of our child. You love and protect us at every moment, and I know they will be proud of you."

"And if they hate me and want me to have nothing to do with you?"

"Luckily for you, this Omega makes her own decision and is mated to the sweetest Alpha on the planet." Dove leaned into her side, nuzzling May's cheek with her nose. She was still getting used to feeling the dormant thrum of May's emotions intertwining with hers. They were told that the dual bite would make the sensation more impactful, and that eventually they could control keeping most everything to themselves, but she would always feel May in her veins. They were one now.

May was nervously worrying her lip and even without the mating bond and the pheromones, it was obvious how anxious she was. She was always desperate to prove herself and Dove would make sure she knew how worthy she was till the end of their days.

Her parents opened the door.

"Dove, you are huge!" her mother Brenda exclaimed, drawing her into a hug and almost setting off a warning from her Alpha. Luckily, Dove was still clutching May's hand, and she sent some calm emotions through their bond.

Dove looked nothing like either of her parents. Her mom had dark brown hair and almost bronze skin, whereas her father had shaggy blond hair and absolutely no freckles. Growing up, she thought maybe they had adopted her, but over the years she realized that genetics were just unpredictable. She hoped their pup would resemble her and May in some way but would love her, nonetheless.

"I really hope that is a compliment, Mother," she mumbled into her mom's neck. Dove had been an only child herself, so her parents were extra cautious of her.

"Of course it is! I have been waiting for the day you would give us our grandpup. I just didn't expect it to be so unconventional." The first jab.

Once her parents found out she was pregnant, they had been breathing down her neck trying to figure out who the Alpha is, since her pheromones took a while to let everyone know who she belonged to. It became clear to them when she moved in with May and her father, Jedediah, almost threatened to pounce on the other Alpha for "knotting" his little girl. Dove promptly shut that down, claiming it was both her decision to not take the herbs and move in with May.

"Well, I am only twenty-nine, Mother." Her gruff father moved past his wife, placing both hands on her shoulders.

"Yes, well, the last time we saw you, you were less pregnant and unmated. It seems your *Alpha* moves fast." Her father bared his teeth at her mate. Dove reached her unoccupied smaller hand out to his wrist to get him to back down.

Logically, Dove knew that her father was just trying to protect her and that his Alpha was trying to convey that, but May's own Alpha was in a state of possessiveness over her newly mated Omega and their unborn pup. Dove hated being the Omega in the middle. She could make her own choices. She always had.

"Both of which were decisions we made together." Dove rubbed her belly over the clothing, drawing May back into her side. "Although, I would prefer to be about ten times lighter." Her pregnancy bump wasn't as prominent as she thought it would be this late into her term, but she was still very clearly pregnant.

"Just imagine if you were carrying two or three of our pups." May's soft whisper brushed her ear. The low humming of May's emotions swam with her own. May was incredibly happy, probably because her Omega's parents were proud of their grandpup.

"It's been quite a while since we've seen you, May." Brenda drew May into a hug, who immediately melted. May hadn't seen her own parents in about five years.

"I apologize for that. I have been so busy with work and settling in." May spoke as Brenda released her from the hug, taking her in.

"Well, that is a bit of a lame excuse. I've been busy making weapons for your soldiers, yet I have time to visit with my daughter and wife every week." Her father butted in. The disappointment in his words created a surge of dismay in the newly mated pairs' bond. Dove pulled her father inside the quarters she grew up in, with her mother and May on her feet. They were out of earshot as Dove led them in.

"Father, May is the Captain of the army. She has duties to our country that we do not. Please take this evening to get to know my mate more instead of berating her, otherwise we will leave." One of Dove's most prominent traits was her ability to be incredibly stubborn, which she got from her father.

"I just think she could have made more of an effort to—"

"Father, I advise you to choose your words very carefully. May has done nothing but provide me with everything even before she found out I was pregnant. There is absolutely no reason for you to dislike her, except you made up your mind that she forced me into this pregnancy when that could not be any other way around. Yet she chose me and does so every day. I will not hear another negative word about my mate and mother of my child, do you understand?"

The old Alpha nodded gently before turning towards the kitchen where the food was being prepared. Even though Dove was a professional cook, she loved when her mother prepared food. Slowly, she went to join her family but stopped when she faced the wall full of old photographs. They ranged from before she was alive to her as a young pup and everything up till today.

She heard her parents and May chattering along in the kitchen, but the pull of her mate brought her out of her memories. She could feel the slight sense of discomfort between their bond.

"May, honey, would you come here please?" The Alpha appeared at her side before Dove blinked.

"What is wrong? Is the pup okay?" May's calloused hands cradled her belly. She was about to drop to her knees like usual when Dove stopped her.

"The pup is fine, honey. I just wanted you to see these." She gestured towards the photographs of her as a young pup. She was probably one or two years old, but she was still dressed in one of her full-body outfits that covered her head to toe. Her parents had called it a onesie at some point since it was one soft cloth. Her dark red waves had started to grow out at that point and her body was covered in freckles.

"You were the cutest pup. I hope our pup has your hair." May loosely twirled a strand of Dove's unkempt hair. She had gone casual with her clothes today since almost nothing fit anymore, and she was uncomfortable in her body. May had been successful in getting her nice fabrics over the past few months that she now wore daily.

"I'll accept the pup having little red locks as long as they are springy curls like yours." Dove took her own finger and pulled one of the light blonde locks to see it bounce back. A low bloom in their bond started growing with each sensitive touch they shared as they gazed upon the photos. It was pure love racing through between them.

"I would like to get our pup an outfit like this one day. Eveleen said that she could get fabric, but the one she adored had a brown cub on the front. I do not want the pup to think it is safe to go around bears." A hand ran up and down Dove's back, her Alpha's soothing gesture causing her to lean into the movement. She could feel May in her cells when she was this close with her. The mate bond, the pheromones, the scent while they touched made them one. Two souls who belonged together, sharing this moment in her childhood home. Dove needed to gaze up into her mate's green eyes. She was whole.

"I don't think the pup will think approaching bears is okay because she has one lined on her newborn clothes. Besides, imagine tickling her little belly while she has a bear protecting her." May's green eyes conveyed the expression that she was imagining it right now. May was amazing at conjuring moments the future family would enjoy together. Dove just listened with openness each time.

"I guess she would look adorable swaddled up in that outfit. I think I would like to dress her up in the cutest clothes we can get our hands on." The Alpha's side of the connection was alive with excitement, bleeding over into Dove. A bright smile grew on her face as May continued discussing clothes for their newborn pup.

Dove felt her parents' gaze, which pulled them both towards the small dining area. Her mate pulled the wooden chair out for her, allowing her swollen body to fit between the table. The Alpha made sure that there was a chalice of water for Dove before gathering up both of their plates to eat the evening meal. Dove's own parents sat across from the newly mated pair.

"So May, it seems like the last time we saw you was before you took over as Army Captain. That was what"—Brenda glanced at her husband—"about four years ago now?"

"Yes, taking over was difficult, but now I am steady and making time for my family." May sliced into some of the food in front of her, taking small bites. Focusing on the conversation and food, Dove was a passive observer. If her father stepped over the line, she would be there for her Alpha, but until then she was happy to see the woman she loved and her parents interacting positively.

"Yes, you have done very well overseeing the troops and coordinating our army. Last time I delivered weapons to the armory, everyone looked well-trained." Her father offered some commentary. The Alpha sat with his shoulders straight while chewing his food. He took each bite with precision as he watched the pair. While his words were not outwardly threatening, they were upsetting enough. Discomfort grew in their bond.

"May is quite excellent at her work, but I would prefer we discuss happier things. How was your trip to the Trilla port?" Dove reached under the table to grip her mate's thigh. May flinched slightly before softening into the touch. They had each other, May had nothing to worry about.

Before long, the conversation settled into an easy talk swapping stories about Dove as a pup and May's own siblings. May told Dove's parents about her older sisters who were born as twins and the younger pair of her brothers, none of whom were drafted, which separated her from her family. May went on to tell them how she stayed in touch with her parents who never felt safe enough to travel out towards the castle.

At one point, Dove's parents questioned if they were going to try for other pups, which pulled a laugh from the very pregnant Dove. The idea of going through these harsh months again made her giggle, but she would love to have duplicates of her and her mate running around someday.

The sun set just after their dessert. Dove's parents brought them over in front of the hearth where something lay under a long linen. There was another box with fancy colored ribbon next to it. Dove bounced on her toes at the sight of presents. She was always excited to receive gifts, but she had a slight suspicion as to what these were.

"What is this?" The questioning tone was directed at her parents, who stood with giddy looks. She felt like a child during the holiday equinox—a hearth full of presents and a happy morning with her family. Dove was excited to experience that with her pup one day.

"You are close to birthing your pup and our first grandpup. We have been so excited to see the day that they are brought home, Dovely." Her mother gathered at one of her sides and her father at the other. "Your father has been working on this for weeks now, and I found something for the pup."

"It is a present?" May broke in on the moment as the newest addition. Jedediah carefully pulled May closer to the happy family. Both Alphas were stiff, but Dove's heart leapt at the thought of them trying to get along.

"I think it would only be fair for each parent to open one, and since Alphas are better, May should get to open the bigger one, wouldn't you agree, Dove?" Her father shot a playful wink between him and May. Dove and her mother, the Omegas in the room, gave a little chuckle. As much as Alphas were the dominant sex, the two in the room were at every whim of their Omegas. Jedediah would do anything for Brenda, and May...May would lay down her life for Dove. Every second that she got to feel May through the bond was another reason to breathe for Dove.

"As if. Omegas are the wiser among the two. Who would keep the primal Alphas in check if not for the

Omegas who could soothe with one use of our pheromones?" Brenda threw back at her husband.

Dove chimed in. "If it wasn't for Omegas, there would be no Alphas around at all. You know, since we are the ones who hold and give birth to your pups." While May was an Alpha, she was also the sweetest and most sensitive person Dove had ever met, and she knew that she was better than any Alphas she met.

"Well then. What do you say, May? Would you like to open the big one or let our sweet Omega do it?" Jedediah presented May with the choice, who looked stunned. Dove made eye contact with her Alpha, who shot a look back with an arched eyebrow. The playfulness of the situation flowed through their bond. Dove almost laughed at the hesitance in May's emotions.

"I would like Dovely to pick which she wants to open." May gestured towards the gifts, presenting Dove with the choice. Dove walked towards the two items, grabbing the linen, unable to resist her excitement. May crowded her space as she took in the gift under it. A wooden, hand-crafted bassinet stood in front of them. The soft furs inside would protect the pup from the cold wood, which she was sure was smoothed to ideal exceptions. The bassinet was curved instead of being rectangular like most. There was a little cover that didn't fully enclose the space and looked like it could be removed. The sides were carved with patterns. And both May and Dove's names were carved near the bottom of the bassinet.

"Father." Dove's lower lip trembled as tears filled her eyes. May stood behind her with her arms loosely wrapped around her. Her light blonde hair tickled Dove as she cried softly at the sight in front of her. May screamed happiness internally, in all forms.

"I was worried it wouldn't be ready in time." His big burly hand landed on May's shoulder. "I think it's time for you to open yours." He handed her the box which May gently opened.

Inside was an outfit for a newborn pup. It didn't have a bear like they had discussed earlier, but there was a little fox tucked in the upper right corner. It was a pale cream color that would not wash out the pup's new skin. May brought it up to her nose and sniffed it cautiously.

"What is the smell?" She brought it close to Dove's nose, who inhaled a little.

"There is lavender, and chamomile infused in the fabric which helps soothe new pup to sleep." Brenda joined them in the gifts. "You two are going to be amazing parents. These are just gifts for you two to excel. Once they are born, we can stitch the name in as well. Have you decided on it yet?"

The lovers met eyes, letting out a joint laugh. They would be good parents indeed, if they could come up with a name.

Chapter 19

A few weeks later, Dove and May discussed at length the conversation May had with their Queen. May had not spoken a single word to Taylor since. Dove and Taylor had had a conversation that lasted a few hours but May hadn't poked in, believing Dove would share if she wanted to.

After a slow morning of making love, Dove had struck up a conversation once May had cooked their morning meal. They sat at the small wooden table with the sun high in the sky. Dove cleared her throat instantly, capturing May's attention. Her posture was rigid with anxiety running through their bond.

"May, I don't want you to be forced to commit treason and I want you to do this before the pup comes." She reached her small hand across the table to capture May's. She was dressed in a light blue chemise that covered her legs. "Just go to town and make sure that it's safe enough. I know you said that some tension may have been relieved with the last council meeting but go see for yourself. You don't even have to tell Taylor why you are going. If you want an excuse, you can get me some stuff for the pup. I've heard they have the perfect ingredients for nausea tea. I would just like to make sure that everything is all right. I know you are upset with Taylor for practically telling you to choose between us and the kingdom, but I know you don't want to bring the pup into the world if there's a uprising brewing." Her hazel, almost gold eyes pleaded with the Alpha. The journey would take all day and if anything happened to Dove, she could feel it in their bond. She wouldn't be able to do anything, and her Alpha would probably haunt her until she saw Dove.

"What if I leave and something happens? You are in the final stage of your pregnancy." She touched on their mating bond. They were mates for almost two weeks now and they were still navigating it. Their souls were intertwined for the rest of their lives. While they didn't share physical pain or thoughts, their emotions were bound together. They could always feel each other and use their emotions to soothe the others. It differed from pheromones because they could do it anywhere and anytime, and others weren't able to see it. Anyone in the vicinity could tap into the pheromones being produced, but no one could touch their bond, making it one of the purest things. If anything was wrong with Dove, May would know.

"How about I spend the day with Eveleen. We can get pampered by the palace staff!" The anxiety from their connection switched from nerves to joy as Dove used her other hand to feel their pup. May wanted to protest that this was her first time off in a while and she would rather remain glued to Dove's side, but she knew that if Dove remained by the other Queen's side, nothing would happen to her Omega.

She had finally rewarded herself with a day off after Caleb and Zoe's return from the ruins. The group that was there seemed to be fighting amongst themselves after the death of their rebel, cause by another. Half of the group was advocating for a violent demand while the other half just wanted an audience with the Queen.

Caleb, Zoe and her other guard members brought back the one's advocating for a meeting, while arresting the others. In the last week, Taylor had meet with more than a few of them to get their account on the rebellion. She heard their demands for the lower taxes and explained her plan to pull from the money she had going toward weaponry. May wasn't particularly happy about it, but it helped soothed some of them. As for the more violent offenders they were going to be put on trial while Taylor tried to gather more information on the rest of the rebel groups.

"Please, May. I do not think I could rest until I know what it's like out there, worrying that Taylor would force you out there while I'm here. I know Taylor. She's our best friend, but if she needs you to step in, she will make you do it. She has to as our Queen." Dove's pleas did not fall on empty ears. This was what Taylor had brought up. It was her duty to the throne. May's boots were by the door, and her cape was hung up on the dresser—she would grab them on the way out.

"You are asking me, she was telling me. I will do this for you, Dovely, but when I come back, I need to rethink my place in the Queen's army." May moved to stand between Dove's parted thighs. Leaning down, she sniffed her Omega's head. The sweet scent of her hair was reassuring enough for May. Dove was safe here.

"If you could tell one of the guards that I want to see Eveleen, then I will stay here and clean up." Dove gathered up their dishes, setting them in the wash basin. May looked around their living space—the furs were scattered everywhere, fresh ingredients were in the kitchen, and their clothing covered most of the bed. She did not want Dove to exert herself, but she would welcome a clean space when she returned. May nodded to Dove in acknowledgement. Once May gathered her boots and cape, she stood by the door.

"I love you, Dovely. I will see you all fresh and pampered when I get back."

"I love you too, May. Bring me back some tea please." May waved goodbye to her mate before leaving the room. First, she went to her office to page Zoe and Kaden, then went up to a guard to relay Dove's message before making her way to the stables. She tried to fend off her worry by remembering who she was in love with. Dove was the strongest person she knew. May knew with their mating, Dove's pregnancy, and the fact she got to be with her sometimes clouded her judgment. Dove was a powerful Omega. May could handle a day away from her mate.

She alerted her guards about the excursion without giving away too much, later finding herself nearing Reverwallow, with her two newest guard members.

Their energy had been off all morning, but she was too focused on Dove during the entire horse ride to care. Her side of the bond was elated as she was with Eveleen, but May could not help but worry. The last time she was here, the Queen was charged and her Omega ended up on the ground instead. If Taylor's audience meeting had had the desired impact, then May hoped word spread to the other rebel groups. Even so, she was glad that Dove was at home, as May contemplated stepping down.

May slowed down to a trot as they neared the entrance gates. "All right, we could be entering a potentially dangerous situation. I know you are both aware of the political tension and today we are going to be here as observers. This is not a mission from the Crown but be aware that some of the civilians could be on edge with our appearance." Zoe nodded, clearly having seen some action in Luiza.

"Is that why we wore our casual dress, Captain?" Kaden's brown hair flowed in the wind. She usually kept it up but it was down in the wind, while Zoe's blonde strands were tucked tightly up.

"Yes, stay by my side." They approached the gates, each dismounting their horses and encountering Reverwallow's guard. With their horses secured after some chatter with her guards, they started walking into town. Since it was nearing dusk, most people were out. May and her newest guard members moved towards the town's center. She noticed a few people that scowled at her and the royal symbol that locked her cape together. Her two companions stood behind her as they walked smoothly through the streets.

"Are you with the royal guard?" A small Beta ran up to May, grabbing the end of her cape. The little boy had blue eyes which twinkled up at her, and shaggy brown curls. He couldn't have been older than six or seven. She bent down to touch the fake wooden sword he was holding. He giggled when she recoiled as if the tip of the blade would hurt her. She wondered where his parents were, but the town had always been safe, at least that's what she knew.

"I am. Did you make this sword yourself?" For a wooden sword it looked pretty accurate. He probably fought with the other young pups that were around. Many people had stopped to watch their interaction. She could see the market area indicating that there were even more people around this area. She would have to be careful with what she said. She had yet to see any signs of unease, but most people were on edge. She could feel it in the air.

"My older brother made it for me. He wanted to join the army when he turned of age." The little boy's scent shifted a bit to sadness. She didn't want to ask about what happened to his brother, but she could sense it wasn't good.

"May I see it?" She opened both her hands with her palms facing upwards. He bit his lip softly before handing over what was probably his most prized possession. He carefully placed the wood in her hands. She could feel Zoe shifting closer to Kaden, but she refused to break the moment with this boy. May turned the sword over in her hands. It had marks that could only be obtained from fighting, but some of the dents showed he was great at defense.

"From the marks on this sword I can see how well of a fighter you are." She handed it back to him and his smile beamed widely. "One day if you want to join, I would be happy to train you." She could sense the shift in the atmosphere, so she turned around. Zoe was practically standing in front of Kaden and growling ahead. May stood instantly, shutting down the other Alpha's protective nature. She had no clue why Zoe would jump in front of her, but she would not have the Alpha causing issues.

May instantly shut it down with her own look. Zoe retreated, taking her place on the other side of May. The little boy had also retreated, probably due to the harshness of her pheromones.

"Zackary!" The Beta's father stormed past the group of bystanders. The number of people had grown exponentially, standing so close they formed a wall. She saw a lot of upset faces. Most of the men had their teeth bared at her and now she could understand the upset looks.

While these people may not be revolting against her currently, they didn't respect her. If she hadn't been so nice to the little Beta, she could imagine them hurting her physically. Instead, she hoped that her actions and words could soothe the growing crowd. Hopefully, they realized she would never work for a dictator who was disguised as a Queen. The sire of the child approached her, so May tucked her hands behind her back.

"My son will never join your Queen's army. He will never rule for a leader who believes in ruthless taxes over her people's living wages. Her audience meeting with the Luiza rebels was just a façade. Nothing has changed!" Zoe stepped up to her left, getting ready to show her fighting spirit, but that was not what May needed right now. She gently put her hand to the side to stop her.

May easily had a few inches on the father, but his upset pheromones overwhelmed hers. She gazed at each of the faces looking at her. Every one of them had their own opinions of her Queen and were forming ones of her. She could tell from their clothes and stature where each person probably ranked in the small town. The man in front of her was highly respected.

"You have nothing to say? You have nothing to say to these people you are meant to protect? The ones who are being bled dry by your Queen." May lifted her chin, trying to weigh her words. These people were angry at Taylor. May was angry at Taylor, but she knew that Taylor only wanted the best for her people. She knew

Taylor's plans were to use the money gathered to grow the economy. The audience meeting may have been one of the first steps in explaining her plans to the rebels, but it was just a week ago. May could see now that the word hadn't spread as widely as she hoped. Now was her chance to educate them on Taylor's plan, but how could she let them know that? She was a fighter, not a speaker.

"Our Queen wants nothing but the best for us." He looked like he was going to swing so she sidestepped him, causing gasps. "I feel that our Queen has not properly spoken on her plan for these taxes, but she has not intended to harm any of you. These taxes were raised to make sure everyone in the land has what they need. They are being used to expand our markets so everyone can sell and buy as they need. Her audience with the rebels was one of many steps she has been executing to make sure everyone is heard, not a façade." Most people were silent as she spoke. They hung onto her words because she had an inside view on the situation. She knew of the uprising, but she knew who her Queen was.

"It may seem like a power imbalance because it has not been explained with the process underway, but this will pave the way for real equality which we need after the devastation the war caused. It will be a stable pathway to making sure everyone can provide for themselves and turn to the kingdom. I understand your doubt, but I would not protect a dictator!" She tried to put every ounce of her morality into the words.

"Then why are you here?" The father seemed calmer than he was a minute ago, as was the crowd. Their faces were twisted in thought as they watched the interaction. Some of them seemed more disgruntled, but the majority were intrigued.

"My mate is pregnant. We came to retrieve some things for her, and I wanted to see the market." Zoe and Kaden moved closer to her as she walked amongst the circle. Someone spoke up but she couldn't see them.

"Do you really believe these taxes are for the best interest of our people?"

"What I believe is that our Queen would never intentionally do anything to harm our people, but some of the rebels acting against the throne are. They have killed people. If you are really concerned about our safety, you would not indulge rebels who want to start a riot against our crown, which will only result in the deaths of our people. Learn from the rebels of Luiza. The only way to real change with our Queen is through talking, not action! She is willing to listen to everyone." She looked towards her guard members. Kaden's face radiated worry and Zoe kept stealing glances at her. She would have to figure it out later. Right now, May had to do her best to speak up for her best friend and her country.

The older Beta who started this approached her with discomfort. "People have really died?"

"Yes." She had nothing more to say. "If you will excuse me and my guards, we will continue our way to the market. I understand your frustration, but there is no world where our Queen would put anyone in harm's way over money, unlike some of the rebels."

She signaled them to follow her as most of the crowd dispersed. She heard the older Beta conversing with some of the bystanders. May felt Dove on the other side of her bond. She was worried for her Alpha and while it made her heart flutter, she didn't want unnecessary distress on her pregnant Omega. May sent back some calming energy, hoping it would help.

"Captain, if I may go look at one of the stands?" Kaden questioned and May gave a silent yes. This would be her chance to question Zoe as they moved to each vendor, but before she could, the older Beta approached the front of the jewelry tent she had been at months before. Zoe sprang into action, straightening next to May. He slowed down but still neared them with a few men behind her.

"Captain. I have been out towards the ruins. We thought the group there was on our side of no violence, but I was unaware they had killed people. Our leaders weren't listening, but I would never be a part of a group that killed someone. We do not want a war. All we want is to make sure each citizen is represented, and safe." He ducked his head at her. He seemed to be in an entirely different state than just moments before.

"I understand. I do not want a war either. I will discuss with our Highness about another open audience meeting. She is always willing to listen but with the recent dispersal of the Luiza rebels, it may be difficult to get a fast meeting." The man looked between his associates as they conversed silently.

"I can get a small group to talk, and have other stand down, if we get an audience with the Queen. I believe we all want the same thing." May's heart stopped. Had this man really just offered to solve her problems without knowing? She glanced at Zoe. The Alpha's golden eyebrow was lifted in shock. She raised her shoulder lightly to signal her own confusion.

"I think that would be an excellent solution to both our problems." May extended her hand. She had some of her guard members took the Beta, who was named Kyle's, information and promised she would contact him in the future. She had to evaluate what had happened here because it was all so overwhelming. She knew there would be a long way to go but if she could start the road to peace, she would take it.

"Thank you for being kind to my son. You will be a great sire." The man ducked away from the conversation, leaving both May and Zoe in front of the stand.

"I think that was what we came to witness, was it not, captain?" Zoe rarely smiled, but when she looked over at Kaden, who was with an older woman, her lips curled slightly.

"Was there a reason you jumped in front of Kaden?" The younger Alpha froze in front of May, darting her eyes between the pair. She wasn't too interested in the pheromones radiating off her, but they penetrated her senses all the same. A mix of nervousness.

"She was suddenly frightened, and my Alpha just sprang into effect. I am aware she can protect herself, but sometimes I lose control around her. I apologize, Captain." Zoe lowered her head, which was when May saw it—a small, bruised kiss mark that was hidden by the golden hairs that sat further back on her shoulders. She didn't mention it but saw Kaden looking at them.

"Do not let it happen again. I will not have either of you in the guard if you feel the need to protect each other. You should be able to protect yourselves." May turned towards the jeweler, but she was happy on the inside.

Even though she saw signs of distress, she also saw an opportunity to create unity again. She could even imagine stepping down as Captain when the situation was averted. A burst of excitement ran through their mating bond. She tried to resist the urge to smile and instead carefully played with the rings in front of her. She recognized the glint of one and immediately purchased it. Maybe Dove was right about this whole idea.

***

When May came home later that evening, she was carrying multiple items. She had plenty of outfits for the pup, a robe for Dove, and a small box.

"I thought you went on a reconnaissance mission, not a shopping mission." Dove's day had been spent with Eveleen getting a full spa treatment. If May found out about the full-body massage though, she might go a bit ballistic, but Dove needed it. She was currently residing on their balcony with the chair facing slightly inward.

"I found a few things for you and the pup." May set down all the small clothes and the robe that looked soft, but not the box. "I also found a potential solution."

Dove's ears perked up. She had tried to ignore May's side of the bond so they could have an afternoon alone, but it was hard sometimes.

"That's amazing. I knew I was secretly a genius." Dove folded the book and set it down before scrambling towards May. She had missed being away from her Alpha for so long. Gently, she put her arms around May's neck.

"You are more than a genius, Dovely." Their lips met in a soft kiss. May moaned against her lips and brought her hands under her belly. She would gently hold it up to relieve the pressure on her back. It was the most soothing feeling she had ever been a part of. Dove's mouth opened and she tipped her head to the side. They continued like that for a few minutes before May broke apart. She grabbed the small box before rejoining her.

"When I was at the market, all I could think about was you. Last time we were there, you were pregnant, but we were not talking. I had left you during your heat, and I will never do that again, Dovely." May grabbed one of Dove's hands before she sank onto one of her knees. "I want the world to know I am yours in every way you will have me. Mother of our child, Alpha, Mate, Wife..." Dove gasped as each of their emotions filled the bond. It created an overwhelming surge in her body. She smiled down at May, who was holding the ring she looked at the last time they were in the market. "I love you, Dove, and I want you to marry me. If you will have me?"

She wanted to sink to her own knees and capture May's lips but since she couldn't, she just pulled her up. "You are everything I've ever wanted, May. Of course I will marry you." She jumped lightly on her feet before May put the ring on her finger and kissed her mating bite.

"You two are my entire world. I cannot wait for you to be my wife."

Chapter 20

With eight weeks left in Dove's pregnancy, May was stretched thin. It wasn't until Caleb confronted her with the offer to help with troop placement that she realized what she needed to do.

After the confrontation in Reverwallow, the man she had come to known as Kyle, met with the Queen twice. The second time he had brought a few men, with one from Sutherland and another from Trilla. Both were highly respected in their village and had gotten their people to listen. The disruption in their country had calmed. Taylor had finally proposed a new system for taxation which would be set into effect at the end of the year. May didn't understand most of the logistics, but she was impressed by her best friend's ability to soothe her kingdom. Taylor's council also helped with the conflict, but May still had her army scattered around the country to make sure the peace stayed. She knew that none of the smaller armies and militias wanted another war, so she banked on the fact that her soldiers would be safe.

Just the night before more of the rebels against the taxation turned themselves in. There would be no death sentence for any except those who killed civilians. The leader of the uprisings had claimed they only wanted proper taxes that were equal for civilians and to gather the Queen's attention. May knew that even though their rebellion was wrong, they all wanted the same thing for their country. She even had multiple communication letters with Kyle who continued talking to the surrounding villages.

Taylor had planned an official council meeting where officials from small villages and towns came to see Taylor sign the new proposal, which the majority agreed with. A few upset voices were expected, but they found it to be fairer than the previous law.

Last night May and Dove had discussed at length about what her position would be now that everything had calmed down.

Dove hadn't necessarily pushed May towards stepping down from her position but bringing it up had been what prompted the chain of events. They laid in bed last night with May gently rubbing Dove's belly while Dove intricately braided her hair.

With just weeks to go, she was enjoying the feeling of her very pregnant mate and their pup. May also enjoyed that Dove finally started nesting and letting herself be doted on. Their souls flowed through each other's veins. May was terrified for their pup to be born and held onto every moment she could.

May stood in front of the door to Taylor's office with the letter in her hand. Raising her fist, she feathered three short knocks on the door. While May trusted Taylor with her life, she felt this moment could also destroy their relationship.

"Enter." Taylor sat with her legs crossed at her desk. May could see why she was Queen. She held so much power in her energy. May had always admired her best friend but now she was viewing her in a different light, which made her nervous. Dove assured her that Taylor would never hate her, but she was in a fragile state lately.

May gripped the paper like a lifeline and entered the royal office. Taylor would understand, right? The Queen's brown eyes gazed at her as she entered the room, a thick silence filling the air. May strode towards the desk, and before she lost the nerve, thrust the parchment in Taylor's direction.

"What's this?" Taylor slowly reached out to grip the parchment that was almost shoved in her face.

"My formal resignation." May stuttered out the words, drawing her hands behind her back. In front of her sat the Queen to her kingdom, the kingdom and country she swore her life to protect. May couldn't do it anymore. Being with Dove, feeling her mate in her helped May realize how amazing she was. Being with Dove was everything May wanted.

"May, what?" The disbelief lined Taylor's voice as she opened the resignation. Dove had helped her the last few days to properly and professionally pen the letter in case Taylor had to present it to her formal council.

"With the pup on the way, I realized I cannot be your Captain anymore. I have asked Caleb, and he would be glad to step up. I know you have the right to say no. I would like to stay on with training, but I cannot keep up with the paperwork and responsibilities anymore, Taylor. My priority is my..." She had yet to say the word to Taylor but now felt like as good a time as ever. "My family." She gulped down the words.

May felt Taylor's gaze burning holes in her skin. Maybe she wouldn't accept the resignation and kick her out of the castle. She had every right. But if May were to leave Dove's side, she would die piece by piece. To be away from her mate would be the cruelest form of torture. She bowed her head, waiting.

"I'm proud of you, May." May gulped down her nerves, unable to meet Taylor's gaze. The younger Alpha's pheromones created a soothing barrier between the two of them, prompting her to continue.

"With the previous unrest, the best way to use me is to recruit and train. I cannot handle the political side, and I have not been able to for a while, but when it comes to training, I can do that. Caleb and I were in discussion, and he said he would be willing to step up if you endorse him. He has been in your army for as long as I have and he is great with the numbers. Me? I have and always will only be a fighter." She kept her gaze on the floor. Her and Dove had discussed this part, about transferring leadership during such a crucial part in their army's history. She wished Dove was here with her, but she felt the support from Dove through their bond. She was in their quarters, preparing things for the pup, and had promised to not think too much into her mate's worries, but May was glad to feel Dove as her lifeline.

"You're wrong, May. You brought forth the solution by forming a bond in Reverwallow. You are a leader, which is why I accept. What we need right now is for people to want to protect our country. There is no better person I trust to fully train recruits and build a solid army for our country, because one day the others may want to invade us in a time of vulnerability." Over the last few months, she had been unable to recognize her best friend, yet as she now sat across from her, she did. Taylor was her sister and the person she could always count on. She may have been the Queen with her duty to the country, but May would always be one of the most important people in Taylor's life. May just needed to remember that.

"Thank you, Taylor." She bowed her head forward, "Maybe you can come over for an evening meal next week, to catch up?" Taylor nodded hesitantly before May promptly left Taylor's office without another word. Because it was one of her off days, she returned to her quarters to find Dove peacefully sleeping on their bed. Per usual she was cradling the pup bump. May walked towards her, kissing the red hairs then making her way to the balcony. She was dressed in a soft robe, as clothes made her feel uncomfortable most days.

They had gotten two velvet chairs and a small wooden table on the balcony recently. Dove had wanted a second bassinet that would protect the pup from the weather as they sat on the balcony. One that would be an outdoor area for the small family. The stone balcony's columns had a few inches between each other and there were about twenty, but May was still worried that the pup would fall through. Dove called her overly cautious, but she was just being protective.

She stared down at the green grass below with the mountains in the distance. On the opposite side of the castle was the land that overlooked the villages. They wouldn't be able to see them, but they could view the plains just before they came into focus. May liked this view better.

On the other side of the mountain was the ocean. May had never seen the ocean. The biggest body of water she saw was a river near her old village. How would she teach her pup to swim? She never had to swim herself, but irrational thoughts hit her. Some of her guards had talked about swimming in the ocean. She continued gazing at the landscape when a pair of arms curled her waist.

"What's bothering you, my mate?" Dove's swollen belly pressed slightly into her back as she placed a few kisses on May's shoulder. The concern laced their bond prompted May to turn around and hold her Omega. She hated when Dove was upset by her own emotions.

"Do you know how to swim?"

Dove's soft laugh filled the atmosphere. She shifted to let May's arms encompass her. Dove's forehead laid freely on May's collarbones. They stood together in a gentle embrace.

"I haven't been by a body of water in a long time, but yes, my parents and Taylor's took us to learn. Why is this coming up?" Dove's body pressed into May. This feeling wouldn't last much longer, but the day she got to hold her pup would change her forever. What if she failed them?

"I do not know how to swim. I was looking out that way and thinking about the things I do not know how to do and everything I want our child to learn." May's hand slid across Dove's stomach. Their child had been moving so often. It was almost like she was ready to be born.

Dove placed both her hands on top of May, stilling her movement. The pup was kicking, making May smile wider than she ever thought was possible. Her cheeks hurt from the crinkling which had been happening very frequently. She was unable to resist when Dove's own glowing skin formed its own smile. Her eyes crinkled in the corners, framing her freckled face magnificently in the early dawn.

"When she is old enough, I'll teach you, my Alpha, and our pup how to swim. What else do you want her to learn?" Before Dove continued the hand movements, she parted her robe, revealing her naked form. Every time May saw it, her Alpha dominated all her senses, lighting up with possessiveness. *She* did that and her Dovely was an angel. Her belly and swollen breasts set May ablaze, and she always let it flow through their bond. Right now, though, she forced her aroused Alpha down just to admire her. Dove let their hands continue moving.

"I was reviewing the list of potential baby names." Dove spoke as May let herself be guided by her mate, dipping their foreheads together. She remained fully dressed as their bodies pressed slightly together.

"I thought you wanted to wait until she was born?" May whispered as their noses brushed. Once again, they both believed the pup was a girl but had picked a whole range of names.

"I saw the one you wrote this morning after you left, and I think it's perfect." The flowing emotions in their connection were driven purely by love. From May's side, she was experiencing every ounce of warmth Dove was feeling. May could feel that Dove almost wanted to purr from joy but was ignoring it.

"Which name?" Every moment with Dove made her heart swell and she never thought it would get better but with their hands still moving in sync along with their hearts, and their foreheads pressed together, she found a new moment that topped all her others.

"Hadley."

Epilogue

May awoke to the soft whispers of her Mate and wife. She was leaning over the bassinet with her hand on Hadley's little tummy. After a grueling eight weeks of maternity leave, the little trio was returning to the real world. Now that May had stepped down as Army Captain and was just a trainer for recruits, she felt the entire weight of that world off her shoulders. All she was concerned with was Dove and their pup. Every day May was lucky to have her two girls, but she believed herself worthy now. Dove and May had had a multi-hour conversation over her insecurity a week after Hadley was born.

"Sorry to wake you. I just fed Hadley, and she looks milk drunk. I have kitchen duty for a few hours and then I'll be back." Dove words were soft when she leaned over to kiss May. Still half asleep, May barely processed the words.

Today was Dove's first day back in the kitchen. She had been out of commission for months and was dying to get back to it. While she had been cooking occasionally for their evening meals, she claimed it wasn't the same. May had planned to get up and help Dove before her duties, but she must have slept in.

"You two girls just sleep." Dove brushed her lips against May's ear. "I love you." May mumbled back before drifting back to sleep.

She woke later from the sun and Hadley's upset cries. Her Alpha jumped into action when her pup started crying. Across the room was the wooden bassinet with the soft, clean fur she had gotten at the market as a present for Hadley.

When May approached, she saw her precious pup swaddled in soft pink. May did not know she could love anyone as much as she loved Dove, and then Hadley came along. She loved them both equally, but it was a different type of love she couldn't describe. It was in a sense that she had never felt as complete as she did when she looked at Dove holding Hadley.

Hadley's cries stopped when her mother appeared over her. It was apparent Hadley had started to recognize her parents, and it made May's heart bloom. What May loved most about her mornings with Hadley was picking her up. The moment before she had her pup in her arms, Hadley's little body scrunched up, as if she was curling into a ball. She couldn't believe one single night with Dove had created her little pup.

"Hello Hadley." May reached one hand out to rub her pup's belly, unaware of how much time had passed since Dove left. The small pup still looked full. Her eyes were the same shade of green as May's. The small head of hair she had was a bit lighter than Dove's own red hair. She was the perfect combination of both of them.

"Are you ready to start the day?" Hadley's tiny tongue popped out of her mouth. May scooped her pup up with both hands to bring her into her body. Warmth filled her. A warm fire at night, nuzzling Dove in bed, hugs from her parents. Nothing compared to having her pup on her chest. Her scent filled her nose. Dove, being the chef and baker, instantly realized how much Hadley smelled like rosemary after she was born. It was faint because she was so tiny, but it was there.

May bounced around the room with Hadley in her arms. She fit comfortably swaddled up against May's warm chest. The small human would never not astonish May. They had created her, and now she got to hold her every day.

The little Omega in her arms was the reason for May to be alive. It was what encouraged her to be her best self every day and the perfect Mate to Dove. She leaned down to kiss Hadley's head, breathing in her scent.

May's official job as army recruiter and trainer led her to have more time with her family and less stress. Her friendship with Taylor was also on the mend. May still sat in on meetings, but she did not have to make the choices. What was best was that the groups that went against the throne were officially disbanded, and Taylor had been working with each town's representative to create change.

The day passed slowly but Dove eventually came back for lunch to feed Hadley, confessing to how much she missed her. They had barely been apart since she was born. May spent the rest of the day reviewing the new training strategy she came up with. She and Hadley took a power nap, lying next to each other in bed, before Dove came home for the evening.

***

When Dove entered her living space, she almost cried with relief. She hadn't realized her first day back involved cooking meals for a hundred people, but Taylor apparently had a big council going on. She ended up been so tired of being around food and was glad that Kelsee had prepared a meal for the new family.

She looked for her Mate and pup but was unable to find them. Concern filled her, but it was quickly shut down when she heard splashing coming from the washroom. She pushed the door open gently to peek at May holding Hadley in the perfect position for a bath. Her heart swelled with emotion. Hadley was still too little for a lot of things, but she was able to push herself up on tummy time. She also loved the water. When she didn't feel well, they would bathe together as a trio. It was some of the most intimate moments of their lives. As a family.

As far as newborns went, Hadley slept through the night fairly well. She slept closest to Dove's side. Sometimes she would wake up to pee in the night and look over Hadley, who slept mostly wrapped up in her swaddle. Taylor had custom ordered the softest cloth for a newborn pup, but it was too big for her because Hadley was very small. She had been born just a few weeks early but was extremely healthy.

"What are my two girls up to?" Dove walked over to kiss May's blonde curls and trail her finger on Hadley's tummy. She hadn't gotten all of Dove's freckles, but she had both of their fair skin. Dove could see how much she looked like May, loving every second of it. Her small nose resembled a tiny version of May's, and the eyes held the same wonder and joy that May had every day.

"Hadley had a little accident, so we took a wash. I think she was getting hungry." May bounced her above the water before blowing kisses on the pup's tummy. Her little giggle filled the air. It was the sound of pure joy. Simple delight in a world where she knew little.

"Well, let's get you both dried off and then we can have a nice evening on the balcony. It's not too chilly out and the sun's setting now." She reached out to take her pup, not caring if she got the slightest bit of water on her. "Hi, my love."

After they were dried, Dove took Hadley with her to the comfy balcony chair and started feeding her pup.

May cut up some of the food to plate it for them. Eventually she found them on the balcony, helping Dove eat. They made small talk about the day, until Hadley slept in Dove's arms. She had been away longer from her pup than she ever had, spending every second craving this moment.

The sun had set, the lantern hanging behind them casting a nice glow along with the moon, while May rambled on about her new plan. Dove would occasionally glance down at her sleeping pup, realizing her wish came true. Here she sat under the stars with the love of her life, and her child. She let out a small laugh, and May gave a soft head tilt before reaching her hand across the table.

"What?" Her side of the bond was as light as ever, and she knew why. When she saw May with Hadley, she was overcome with joy. Dove would never be able to describe the feeling, yet she craved it every day.

"I always knew one day you would have a pup, and I would hope to have my own, but I never knew that she would be ours and it has been better than I expected." She gazed down at Hadley.

"I'm excited to spend the rest of my life with you." May's smile was pure as she spoke back.

"She may have been an accident, but she brought me everything I ever needed." With that, May leaned over and kissed her before they looked at the stars, Hadley tucked into their sides.

THE END

Acknowledgements

Thank you to Lily for not only introducing me to the omegaverse but inspiring me to write my own and for answering all my questions.

Thank you to Morgan, my beta reader who loves these two as much as I do. For engaging in a silly book that started a joke and ended up becoming a whole universe. For also recommending the OV to me. This story would not have made it this far without you.

Thank you to Victoria and Alora who fought over who would be the first to read it. I love you guys so much. As well as my Lyssa's and Lissa's

Thank you to Luna, CC and CR for helping me through the process. To Elizabeth and Danny who indulged a 17-year-old me with the most ridiculous idea. You were the first to ever read what I wrote. Thank you to my family and my best friends.

Thank you to the person who asked for a list of sapphic omegaverse, because without that google search this book would not exist.

Thank you to NK for making May Dove and Hadley come to life. To see my characters on the cover was a feeling I'll never forget. And to Saumya for the beautiful world of Whaow Frar. For Caitlin for helping me so much with everything.

Thank you to my editor. Sorry that I didn't believe in commas!

Finally, thank you to everyone who gave May and Dove and me a chance.